Kick-ass Mules

John Cobb

Introduction

"Kick-ass Mules" takes a colorful look back at the 1970's through the lens of Division III football. It is loosely based upon my life experiences at Muhlenberg College and takes place between November 1972 and December 1973. While the story revolves around the game of football; the music, current events, and pop culture of the times are just as significant to the reader's enjoyment. It's a fun, nostalgic ride through the early seventies when we were all a bit more naïve and flourished with less rules and more societal leeway. Where possible the language and slang of that era are incorporated into the characters' dialogue.

Another key aspect is my love of Division III football and the realization that the commitment it takes to play the game at that level is similar to D-I. The players at the top rung are bigger and faster with better equipment but the end goal is the same. Players have to prepare themselves mentally and physically to endure the rigors of the game towards the pursuit of excellence.

The themes of perseverance and teamwork are prevalent throughout the book. It was important that the 1973 Muhlenberg Mules put behind them the failures of the previous campaign and move forward. By bonding at the Jersey Shore during the summer of '73, a core group learned to trust and depend on each other. We translated that to success on the field while having plenty of fun along the way. This is our story which can best be described as "Animal House" meets "Forest Gump".

Dedications

First and foremost I dedicate this book to my family who have always been there for me and have had a major influence on my work ethic and life values. My mother, Margaret; father, Charles; sister, Lori; and wife, Debbie, are loosely represented as characters in "Kick-ass Mules". In fact I met Debbie at Muhlenberg College and we married at the school chapel in 1978.

My children Tyler, Lacey, Brady and Hunter, along with *our* grandchild Charlie, make me smile on a daily basis. Their unconditional love and creative spirits are the centerpiece of my world and influence all aspects of my life. They make every day I spend with them a loving adventure and their "Old Man tweets" keep my ego in check.

My appreciation to Kasey Barrett, a talented artist and designer in Minneapolis who created the cover and gave my book a face. I am in awe of her creative spirit and passion for her craft.

Additionally I want to recognize one of my roommates at Muhlenberg College, Jim Gaydos. He passed away much too early at the age of sixty just prior to the initial release of this book. The character Jim "Tasmanian Devil" Shapiro is based upon my former roommate and friend. His intensity and dedication made him a conference wrestling champion for Muhlenberg. While I admired him for those traits it was his ability to make me laugh that I will forever miss. Whether it was his expressive tantrums, or his infectious grin, he never failed to crack me up.

I still remember vividly the time he could not figure out why he smelled bad after taking a shower. It was making him crazy and he hounded everyone in the dorm to smell him to see if he was the culprit or if the musty odor was just a figment of his imagination. After we let him rant for a while I finally said to Jim, "Get rid of that rancid shoebox that you are holding. That is what stinks...not you." Jim kept all his toiletries in an old cardboard tote. As usual, it ended with Jim flipping out and chasing us around the room with his smelly box while we laughed our balls off.

I would be remiss not to mention all the coaches and teammates I played with at Muhlenberg College and Hunterdon Central High School. I enjoyed every minute of the journeys we embarked on and it was the friendship and camaraderie that meant the most to me regardless of the won – loss records. It was the shared experience of enduring tough summer workouts and challenging fall practices that made us appreciate going through it as a team. We laughed together, cried together and ultimately succeeded together. The coaches I had the privilege to play for were great role models and taught us valuable life lessons about hard work, commitment to a cause and having fun along the way.

Lastly, I want to pay my respects to all the individuals past and present that play Division III football. There are no scholarships, no 80,000-seat stadiums, and no television contracts. You play football for the purest motivation....for the genuine love of the game. I salute your passion and intensity. Remember to savor the experiences and cherish the relationships you develop along the way. The competition goes by all too fast but the memories get bigger and better with each passing year.

Kick-ass Mules

CHAPTER 1   "You're outta here"

The frat party band is doing their best rendition of Humble Pie's, I Don't Need No Doctor...

> *"I don't need no doctor*
> *'Cause I know what's ailing me*
> *I don't need no doctor*
> *'Cause I know what's ailing me*
> *All I need is my baby*
> *You don't know I'm in misery*
> *I don't need no doctor*
> *I don't need no doctor................."*

While I sit in the corner of ATO's basement contemplating today's season-ending 38-14 loss to Moravian College, it appears most have moved on with the help of beer and grain alcohol. I guess the result shouldn't surprise anyone if you consider the team mascots. Moravian is represented by a Greyhound—a slender, graceful and fast pedigreed dog, while Muhlenberg's mascot is a mule....a jackass. Essentially a hybrid between a donkey and a horse meant for hard labor—the opposite of sleek. But what mules possess are a capacity for work and a stubbornness that remains undeterred in the face of obstacles. They are highly regarded for their stamina, strength, and intelligence.

Tougher than horses and smarter than donkeys, there is a reason they are relied upon to get the job done.

Being a one-hundred and eighty-five pound, undersized guard/linebacker, I identify with the mule. I was not particularly fast, graceful or big. The first time my Line Coach, Sam Ballzano, (Coach Balls behind his back....Coach Sam to his face) saw me practice he said, "Cobber, you may not be big but you aren't fast either."

Coach Balls was a real piece of work. Two-hundred and eighty-five pounds sitting atop a five-foot, eleven inch round-frame and the biggest butt you ever saw. His ass was so big it had its own zip code. He played defensive tackle for Muhlenberg back in the sixties and holds the longest fumble recovery on record at seventy-five yards. Seeing Coach Balls today I can't imagine him running that far without stopping to take a cigarette break (his vice of choice). The opponents from Lebanon Valley must have stopped running after Coach Balls and started a betting pool as to which yard line he'd fall down on in exhaustion. In spite of his gruff behavior and arrogance, I thoroughly enjoyed playing for Coach Sam. His verbal assault was his way of keeping everybody loose and once you gained his respect, he always had your back. On a regular basis he chewed us out but under his surly demeanor he cared deeply about "his guys".

Another of his favorite tactics was to push hard on the freshmen players. Coach would shout in my face, "Remember your place Cobber! You are like whale shit on the bottom of the ocean!" Encouraging words for a rookie from Whitehouse, New Jersey, but they only made me more determined to succeed.

My modus operandi was to work as hard as I could on or off the field. Whether it was mental or physical preparation, I made sure when my number was called I was ready to compete. Work ethic was a core value I inherited from my parents. Given my limited athletic prowess it was my only competitive advantage.

Rehashing today's game, my roommate, Terry "the Tank" Destefano, a 265 lb. tackle on the team tried to make me feel better. "Cobber you really fucked up that kid today good on the kick-off, you know. We lost the game but you got a pound of flesh. Coach Balls was so pissed! How does it feel to get kicked out of the game in front of everyone?"

Tank wasn't the only one patting me on the back and congratulating me for getting tossed out of the game. Being a sophomore that only plays on the bomb squads, I have to admit the recognition did feel pretty good— even if it was for a screwed-up reason. But late in the fourth quarter as we were finishing off a 1-8 season, I see one of my teammates, #67 Chuck Biers, get hit in the back on a 4th quarter kickoff return. I saw red. At the end of the play, in the middle of the pile of human flesh, I go after the Moravian player and attempt to detach his head from his body. My hands are completely locked on his facemask making every effort to twist off the helmet with his head in it. My teammates and I had recently seen The Godfather movie and subconsciously I think I wanted to reprise the bedroom horsehead scene with a Greyhound beheaded in the middle of Bethlehem, Pennsylvania. Before I could complete my decapitation, I was grabbed by a mixture of Muhlenberg and Moravian players as the head official shouted, "You're outta here!"

"Tank, I'm not proud of getting my ass kicked out of the game but I just sorta lost control when Chuck got speared from behind. Coach Balls will never let me forget this. Can you imagine how much fuckin' running I'll have to do next season as punishment?"

"Don't sweat it now roomie, we have a whole nine months before next season starts," says Tank.

"Well I tell you one thing Big Man, I don't intend to remain a loser. Whatever it takes we need to sacrifice cause I don't want to feel like dogshit this time next year. Hey who is that girl with the arrows all over her shirt?"

"That's Debbie D'Angelo, a freshman from North Jersey. Don't waste your time. She has a hometown and doesn't dig jocks. She hangs out with the brainiacs from Zeta Beta Tau."

Despite Tank's lack of encouragement I could not get this girl out of my head. Debbie was 5-feet, five inches of pure gorgeous with beautiful olive skin and dancer's legs. With a flash of her smile Debbie could persuade a devout vegetarian to eat a cow. Her hour-glass figure was busting out of the shortest denim short-shorts I'd ever seen and her ample rack was testing the limits of her arrow-designed tank top. Her parents gave her appropriate initials with "DD" since the Lord blessed her in the cleavage department.

As the band takes a break, the sound system plays David Bowie's "Changes":

> *"Still don't know what I was waitin' for*
> *And my time was runnin' wild*
> *A million dead end streets and*
> *Every time I thought I'd got it made*
> *It seemed the taste was not so sweet*
> *So I turned myself to face me*
> *But I've never caught a glimpse of*
> *How the others must see the faker*
> *I'm much too fast to take that test*
>
> *Ch-ch-ch-ch-changes*
> *Turn and face the strange*
> *Ch-ch-changes"*

I lose sight of Debbie and my mind turns to the changes the Mules will need to make if we're going to transform into a winning unit.

It's now close to 2:00 AM, and two of my buddies try their best to get me up to my room. Jim Shapiro and Greg Wolfe are both on the wrestling team. Shapiro, nicknamed the Tasmanian Devil for his continuous motion on the mat was the 134 lb. Mid-Atlantic Conference Champ as a freshman last year and Greg the "Wolfman" was our starting 148-pounder. Jim and Greg clamp a few wrestling holds on me and forcibly escort me up the back stairs of our four-story, English Tudor frat house. It must have taken them fifteen minutes to cover the 30 steps upstairs. Once I got to the top of the stairs, a surge of power overtook me. No doubt the result of a dozen beers and multiple grain alcohol fruit punches I drank this evening to erase the memories of our most recent defeat.

I break free from both guys and proclaim in my loudest voice, "I am Superman!" and jump off the top step onto the cement steps below. As I lay bleeding on one of the landing areas, I have no comprehension of what I've done or why. And definitely not sober enough to appreciate how lucky I am to be alive or at the very least without a broken neck. Tasmanian Devil is surveying the damage and proclaims to Wolfman and a few others near the back stairs, "He's bleeding from his forehead and I think he knocked himself unconscious!"

I later learned I was out for about a minute or two, but luckily our Frat President (nicknamed Candy Man) had a girlfriend studying nursing at Allentown General Hospital who came to my aid. Susie was truly my Florence Nightingale. She stopped the bleeding and checked for signs of neck and spinal damage. As I become stable, Susie and friends helped me to the Student Health Center.

After four stitches and observation for concussive injuries I finally got into bed at the frat about 6:00 AM that morning with a badly bruised face and one black eye. At least I was (barely) in one piece.

Chapter Two

"Acorns don't fall far from the tree"

With my parents coming up this weekend for a visit, I had to come up with a good story to explain the black eye. Telling Jenny and Ken Cobb that I got stinking drunk and tried to fly down the backstairs wouldn't go over well. They are no-nonsense folks. My Mom was raised on a farm, and my Dad, without a formal education, built a very successful chain of pet stores known as Try-Cob Inc. If you look in the dictionary under perseverance you see photos of Jenny and Ken Cobb.

One of my Dad's favorite sayings was, "Acorns don't fall far from the tree." This was especially true for my sister, Judy. She was a tiny blond dynamo that never backed down to anyone, especially me. Our fights growing up were legendary. Despite being two years younger and probably eighty pounds lighter, Judy held her own. I was on the receiving end of her razor-sharp teeth and nails many times as we were growing up. I think she filed her teeth to points to get better penetration on my arms and legs. The blood-letting, bedroom battles only heightened my admiration for her toughness. While we scrapped with each other, we couldn't be closer. Judy is one of the most determined, loving and focused human beings God has ever placed on this earth. She could do anything she put her mind to.

With Mom and Dad scheduled to arrive on the Muhlenberg College campus in six days, I was still searching for a plausible explanation for my black eye and stitches. They were proud of me when I choose to attend 'Berg and I didn't want them to question my selection.

Muhlenberg College, founded in 1848, is a small, liberal arts college located in Allentown, Pennsylvania. The city represents a hardworking community with a blue collar attitude known for its iron, railroad and beer brewing industries.

Muhlenberg's campus is located in a quiet residential neighborhood in Allentown's West End and spans eighty-one acres. What struck me the first time I set foot on campus were the numerous brick and stone buildings with distinctive red doors. The two most impressive buildings reside in the middle of the campus. The Library Building, built in mid-1920 is home to a distinctive dome and tower. It was inspired by Oxford University's famous bell tower, Tom Tower. The Egner Chapel, constructed a few years after the Library, is a soaring gothic structure of limestone and granite with interior dimensions rising 150 feet surrounded by stunning stained-glass windows.

Due to the fact that Muhlenberg College is 55 miles north of Philadelphia, 90 miles west of New York City and 40 miles west of central Jersey, the vast majority of football recruits come from the tri-state area.

My Dad was sold on me going to Muhlenberg on our first visit when he met Coach Sam and Head Football Coach, Ed Marino. Coaches Ballzano and Marino practiced good cop/bad cop with Coach Balls handling the negative side of that equation. I remember Dad saying in his initial meeting with Coach Sam, "Don't be afraid to work his ass off" and "if he gives you any back talk, I want to know about it."

I don't think Coach Balls needs any encouragement Dad.

The two of them bonded and Dad was convinced that Coach Sam would provide the right level of discipline and structure. His gut feelings, much to my chagrin, proved accurate.

Saturday morning rolls around, and I hear Dad from the front lobby of the ATO house. "Can you tell me where Jack Cobb is?"

Here goes nothing. I hope they buy my excuse.

I rush to throw my arms around Mom to avoid her looking directly at my facial wounds. "Hey Mom and Dad, how are you?"

"What's the matter with your eye and your head?!?" exclaimed Mom.

"Well, it's a long story."

"We have time.....we just got here," Dad adds.

At that moment a special announcement came across the living room TV:

> "Whitehouse Press Secretary Ron Ziegler communicated today that there will be no more public announcements concerning United States troop withdrawals from Vietnam because troop levels are now down to 27,000."

The Vietnam War finally appears to be winding down after more than a dozen years of bitter conflict and tremendous loss of life.

> *Man, am I glad my draft lottery number never got called. I'm one lucky son-of-a-bitch.*

I attempt to redirect Dad to the TV, but he's not biting. "Forget the boob tube, how did you hurt yourself?"

"Well you know how much I like wrestling. Greg and I were messing around near the front stairs and he got a good upper body throw on me. I hit the railing and a step on the way down. I'm fine now. Nothing to worry about. Stitches are out and my eyesight is 20/20."

Thankfully they bought it, but from that moment on, my mother gave the evil eye to Greg whenever she saw him the entire weekend. While my mother was one of the most loving people you could meet, if she thought you wronged one of her family members she'd turn on you like a momma bear protecting her cubs.

I was sorry I had to throw Greg under the bus with my made-up excuse, but occasionally a few have to be sacrificed for the good of the whole. It was Greg's turn to be noble, but regrettably it would be years before Mom would smile at Greg again.

My face was not the only topic of conversation I needed to explain to my parents. My mid-terms arrived this week:

Microeconomics – D
Spanish – D
Labor Law – C
Russian Literature – B

Principles of Economics – C

Apparently the strong work ethic I received from my parents was more visible on the field than the classroom. They wouldn't be happy given the fact I had somehow made the National Honor Society back at Hunterdon Central High School.

As we sat down for a nice lunch at the Shanty Bar and Restaurant out on 19th Street, I broached the subject of the mid-terms.

"My mid-term grades arrived this week. It's been a struggle with my coursework this semester with foot…"

"Stop right there son. Never use football as an excuse for bad grades. Plenty of your teammates handle both responsibilities well. You are just not using your time effectively. Show me the grades."

> *He's got me dead nuts on. Just shut up and take the pounding.*

After viewing the grade summary with a clinched chin, Dad says firmly, "You need to focus your attention and get those grades up by semester's end. There is no reason you can't have all Bs at the very least. I'm not paying $3,000 a year tuition for you to have a good time."

> *In actuality I received a $500 loan and a $500 scholarship each year so it is only $2,000, but now doesn't seem to be the time to correct him.*

Mom tries to deflect the conversation. "Ken you made your point. Let's enjoy the meal and our time with Jack."

"Okay Dad, I'll buckle down. Try your burger, you don't want it to get cold."

The Shanty Bar was usually a sanctuary where I relaxed and enjoyed the company of my frat brothers on most Thursday nights, but today it felt more like an inquisition. However I had no excuse not to buckle down. The football season was ending and I needed to get my ass in gear.

Chapter Three

"A match made with Mono"

It's mid-November and my birthday was coming up on the 22nd. I'm a classic Scorpio: intense, with a passion for life and an ease with expressing emotions. I had recently been following along with the triumphs of a fellow Scorpio athlete, US Open Ladies Champion, Billie Jean King. She's the embodiment of toughness with her aggressive style of play, and already owns nine individual Grand Slam titles at age 29. The Mules could use an infusion of her competitive spirit.

Pisces are said to be good romantic matches for Scorpios, and as luck would have it the girl at the frat party, Debbie D'Angelo, was just that. Up to this point, I'd only had a few brief, passing conversations with her. But today, things changed. As I tended to my campus job as a food runner for the Student Health Center, I received the opening I'd been looking for.

I knocked quietly and entered patient room #3 with a tray of food. What do my eyes behold but Debbie D'Angelo herself.

I try my best to be casual. "Hey Debbie, what's going down? I'm surprised to see you."

"Not as surprised as I am. I had no idea you work as a food runner. I'm so embarrassed to see anyone in this condition. I got mono a week ago and I've been fighting it ever since. I must look a mess."

"You look fine to me," I reply with a smile.

*That's the best line you could come up with,
Dumb Ass?*

"Thanks, but I know I look like road kill. At least that's
what I feel like. Do you mind turning down the TV?"

*Now that's a good sign. She wants the TV lower
so we can talk, at least I think that's what she
means.*

All in the Family is playing and I resist the temptation to
laugh as Archie blasts Meathead. With the TV volume as
low as I could possibly make it without turning it off
completely, I began to lay out Debbie's food. Usually I
can be in and out of a room in ten minutes. Today I've no
such desire to be expeditious. I methodically pull out the
mobile table, painstakingly square up the white
tablecloth and meticulously lay out her dinner one item,
one utensil at a time. I excuse myself and frantically run
out to the lobby to use the phone.

As fast as I can, I dial the cafeteria and ask to speak to
another food runner. To my fortunate surprise, my good
buddy, Arnie Palmisano, answers. He's the Mules
quarterback and his twin brother Paul is our tight end.
They're from Frenchtown, New Jersey, and played at my
high school's rival in the Delaware River Conference.
Despite the Twins' best efforts, my Hunterdon Central
Red Devils beat the Del Val Dawgs all four years.

"Arnie, I need you to do me a solid. Something has come
up and I can't get back to the Student Union. Can you
take my runs? I'll owe you."

"What's the chick's name, dingus?" He asks with a fair
amount of snark in his voice.

Not feeling very talkative I snap back, "Don't give me shit right now. Can you do it or not?"

"Don't get your panties in a bunch, ass breath. I just finished my shift. I'll cover you."

"Fan-fucking-tastic! I owe you bro. Thanks." Feeling euphoric about my pending encounter with the girl of my dreams, anticipation starts to swell within me.

I pass a mirror on the way back to Debbie's room and make my best effort to brush back my disheveled hair with my hands. Just before entering the room, I wet my fingers with my lips and pat down my Fu Manchu mustache one last time.

"Sorry, I just had to check if you're my last run."

"Is it your last stop?"

I nod, trying keep my nerves from kicking in. "Yeah, I'm done for the day."

"Can you stay and talk awhile?" she asked.

I quickly blurted out, "Yeah, I already finished my studying. I can stay for as long as you want."

Who am I kidding? I didn't study shit today.

Debbie smiled and added, "That's great. I enjoy the company and TV's boring."

She motioned for me to take a spot on the bed since there wasn't even a chair in this extremely small patient room. I carefully hop-up on the end of the bed.

How good is this? The girl I've been trying to talk to is now a captive audience. She can't run away this time.

Debbie may have mono, but damn she looks great to me. Despite being clad in red flannel pajamas, she can't hide her curvaceous figure. And her enchanting brown eyes keep me fixated on her every word.

We end up talking for over two hours about everything from our interests to what our childhoods were like. Debbie is a psychology major and 'Berg cheerleader who enjoys dancing and gymnastics. She's also co-captain of the Modern Dance Team. But two issues gave me cause for concern. One, she has a hometown boyfriend back in Bergen County, NJ and two, her parents live in an upscale, affluent, neighborhood. I'm from a modest, farming community within rural Hunterdon County. Was it possible this could be the start of something, despite our different backgrounds?

I remained convinced we're good for each other, and make a vow to myself to make Debbie forget her hometown guy after Christmas break when she recovers.

Chapter Four

"The concert ends on a tragic note"

It's a cool late-November morning and I'm jacked Billy Joel is coming to campus this Saturday to perform a gig at our Fieldhouse. He played a couple of times in the Allentown area over the past year. Last summer I attended his show at the Allentown Fairgrounds and Billy blew me away. Lately there has been a lot of buzz around him because an FM radio station in Philadelphia, WMMR has been playing his song, Captain Jack, regularly and his popularity is spreading nationally.

This Saturday is going to be a stone-cold groove.

As I finish a morning four-mile run, I stop to admire the ATO frat house. It's a grand old building with tremendous character. A distinctive three-story, English Tudor dominated by brick walls and timber beams. An enormous stone chimney dominates the left side of the property with multiple gables forming the roof line. My bedroom window opens up over the multi-level roof. On many a sunny, spring day my buddies and I hang out there with a few Iron Cities checking out the 'Berg babes. The inside is just as cool with a huge dining hall where we host parties, a comfy TV room with a large stone fireplace, a rec room equipped with pool and ping pong tables and a kitchen for our in-house cook. We even have a secret meeting room used only for the most important of frat activities like new member initiation ceremonies.

Part of the basement is dedicated to weightlifting. Several athletes live in the house and we're lucky that three of them keep their ample supply of free weights there. The trio is quite a contrast in personalities and body types, but they share a love of pumping iron. Scott Cressman is a six-foot, one-inch, two-hundred and thirty pound discus thrower on the track team with shoulder-length locks from outside Philadelphia. I refer to Scott as our prize hog since he's an underclassman and we need to maintain mental domination over the youngsters until they develop social skills. It was our duty as upperclassmen to serve as mentors to the unenlightened and inexperienced.

Burt Massa is a five-foot, three-inch, two-hundred pound, power-lifter from South Plainfield, New Jersey. Burt is literally a barrel with four stubs for arms and legs. God made him for powerlifting. Before our eyes, he has bench pressed close to five hundred pounds! Burt takes a lot of crap as an ATO officer because he's so fastidious and neat. If you want to bust his balls just make a mess somewhere in the house. Burt will immediately tweak out, much to our delight.

And last is Steve Holland who's a starter on the wrestling team at one-hundred and ninety pounds as well as the President of our Fellowship of Christian Athletes Chapter. His nickname is "Preacher" because he constantly reminds us there is a higher power we need to embrace, and we are thankful he does because we spend a good portion of our energy acting like self-centered assholes, albeit well-meaning assholes.

The reason I pledged ATO during my freshman year was because the brothers I met during rush represented all different types of personalities. ATO had jocks, heads, nerds, preps, geeks, brains, fuck-ups and suck-ups. You name it, we had it. This eclectic group of characters with nicknames like, Ads, Candy Man, Boose, Helmo, Doc, Landru, Ensign, Corny, Chico, and Bone made a great, college family with very different strengths and full of idiosyncrasies.

It's late in the afternoon and most of the guys in the house are getting ready for the Billy Joel concert that's slated to start in about three hours. I jump in my 1960 white convertible Cadillac with my roommate Tank, and make a sandwich run to George's Deli. Despite the Caddy being thirteen years old, it's a sweet ride. Large white walls, big fins in the rear and enough chrome on the front grill to comb your hair in. The only downside is that my car eats gas getting only about ten miles to the gallon. As I pass Joe's Esso Station that point is hammered home, seeing prices rising to fifty-five cents a gallon.

Will gas ever stop going up?

With sandwiches in hand we return to the frat house and chow down in the living room watching a TV re-run of Bonanza. Hoss is beating up three bad guys that pistol-whipped Little Joe, while our frat brothers start to assemble around us. It feels like the calm before the storm as we sense the excitement build in the room. Scotty Freed, a free spirit with a head full of shoulder-length curls who looks identical to the lead actor in the movie Jesus Christ Superstar, is playing a fake air piano and singing one of Billy Joel's staples:

"But Captain Jack will get you high tonight
And take you to your special island
Captain Jack will get you by tonight
Just a little push 'n' you'll be smilin'
Oh yeah, yeah"

The Dalsey Twins join Scotty, busting out the lyrics at the top of their lungs. The atmosphere is balls-out energy.

It's time for the show!

The Muhlenberg Fieldhouse holds about three thousand people, and every spot on the floor and bleachers is taken. The enormous stage gives Billy Joel the opportunity to run from one side of the building to the other. I'm sitting next to Tank, the Palmisano Twins and Sam Johnson, a guard on the football team from Norwich, New York. Sam and I are kindred spirits since we both came to Muhlenberg the same year as undersized guards and immediately created a bond with each other. Next to Sam are three of our ATO Little Sisters; Sandy, Peggy and Sue—all groovy Jersey chicks.

As Billy Joel enters the stage from the back he shouts "What's shaking, Muhlenberg?", and the place erupts in a crescendo of shouts and applause. His initial song is one of my favorites, Only the Good Die Young.

"Come out Virginia, don`t let me wait
You Catholic girls start much too late
aw But sooner or later it comes down to fate
I might as well be the one...

Well, they showed you a statue, told you to pray
They built you a temple and locked you away

Aw, but they never told you the price that you pay
For things that you might have done.....
Only the good die young
thats what i said
only the good die young"

Sandy jumps up on Sam's back as the entire crowd is on their feet dancing and singing along with Billy. His energy level is off-the-charts. He continues to play for three and a half hours with four encores. My only regret is that Debbie isn't there to enjoy the concert with me. She's still recovering in the student health center from her bout with mono.

After the show a bunch of us go over to Lambda Chi, location of the after party. Their frat house is a short walk from ATO and the kegs are on tap in the basement. It's a cozy place—if you don't mind black cement floors usually covered in two inches of beer. I've spent many an hour there because a large number of our football teammates are brothers of Lambda Chi.

Tank stumbles up to me and feeling no pain shouts, "Ah Cobber, like... let's blow this taco stand. I hear there's a happening time going on at Martin Luther, ya know."

Martin Luther is an ivy-laden, brick residence hall that is part of "The Quad" in the middle of campus. My suspicion is that Tank just wants to meet up with Rosy, a girl he's been dating on and off since the beginning of the year. Rosy bears a striking resemblance to Popeye's girlfriend, Olive Oil but much prettier: tall, long limbed, about one-hundred and five pounds soaking wet and stylish, short brown hair. Rosy is so thin that when she eats a candy bar it looks like a mouse going through a boa constricter.

"Don't have a cow,Tank. Let's have one more for the road and enjoy the tunes," I said.

"Fuck beer! I wanna goooo...Martin Luther," roars Tank in an ever increasingly incoherent manner.

"Take a chill pill, Big Man. Let me finish this beer and we'll go. Two minutes."

"Like ahhhh alright, Cornhole, drink yourrrrr, goddamn beeerrr," bellows Tank as he releases an atomic belch in my face.

Cornhole is a nickname guys use when they want to piss me off. I prefer Cobber or Cobby—definitely not Cornhole.

"Now that I have your fucking DNA all over me, let's go." My face curls a little in disgust as I wipe away the remains of Tank's rancid burp off my face with a bar napkin.

As we approach the Quad from Lambda Chi, it's filled with students still buzzing from the concert. There's at least a couple hundred people digging the scene. Someone's sound system is setup in a nearby window playing the Eagles.

> *"Well, I'm running down the road*
> *tryin' to loosen my load*
> *I've got seven women on*
> *my mind,*
> *Four that wanna own me,*

Two that wanna stone me,
One says she's a friend of mine
Take It easy, take it easy
Don't let the sound of your own wheels
drive you crazy"

As we get close to the building, we notice Sam Johnson teetering on a narrow ledge adjacent to the roof. Sam is all about pushing boundaries and has somehow gotten past a locked door. Before any of us are able to coax him off the roof, Sam loses his footing and falls thirty feet onto a brick walkway. The horrific fall takes place in the blink of an eye and places the Quad crowd in a collective state of shock. Chaotic shouts and cries overtake the music as a number of us rush to his aid.

Frankie Johnson, our All Conference defensive end runs to the nearest door to call 9-1-1 from the lobby phone. Meanwhile, Tank and I try to do what we can for Sam but he's not responding despite our efforts to revive him. Never before had I seen anybody that hurt up close. My heart is beating out of my chest as we attempt to determine if Sam is breathing. Tank detects a pulse at his wrist and Sam's chest is moving up and down. Our friend is breathing on his own with a pulse. I silently thank God over and over.

I couldn't comprehend what had just happened. Only a few short hours ago Sam, Tank and I were shoulder to shoulder, boogieing to Billy Joel on the Fieldhouse floor. Now our brother lies motionless out in the Quad. I'm totally freaked out as emotions overwhelm me. Doing our best to fight back tears, Tank and I console Sam and whisper, "It's gonna be OK. Hang in there buddy." Sam wasn't responding.

It *looked bad...real bad.*

Luckily it appeared Sam fell on his side, so neither his back nor his front absorbed the full impact. The Allentown Rescue Squad arrived on the scene within five minutes. The EMTs only allowed Gina, Sam's girlfriend to ride in the ambulance. As it took off we make plans to drive to Allentown General Hospital.

It's after midnight and the emergency waiting room is filled with Muhlenberg students and faculty. It doesn't take long for the bad news to travel. Coach Sam and Coach Marino are also in the reception area waiting to hear any news on how Sam is doing.

A nurse came out and spoke to Coach Marino, "Sam will be in surgery and recovery for hours. You all might as well go home and get some sleep. You can't do anything tonight. We'll know more in the morning."

Coach Marino has the unenviable task of calling Sam's parents to inform them of his accident. We learn later that Sam's parents drove through the night to arrive at the hospital the next day.

After Coach Marino shares the nurse's information with us, a number of students leave for the night. About a dozen of us decide to sleep in the waiting room should any news come earlier.

Preacher gets us in a circle holding hands and begins praying.

"Lord, look upon Sam with the eyes of your mercy. We entrust him to your care this night. We turn to you for strength. May your love and joy flow through us to heal Sam."

Then he recites Psalm 23 as we join in intermittently.

"The LORD is my shepherd; I shall not want.
He maketh me to lie down in **green pastures**:
He leadeth me beside the still waters.
He restoreth my soul:
He leadeth me in the paths of **righteousness** for his name's sake.
Yea, though I walk through the valley of the shadow of death,
I will fear no evil: for **thou art** with me;
Thy rod and thy staff they comfort me.
Thou preparest a table before me in the presence of mine enemies:
Thou anointest my head with oil; my cup runneth over.
Surely goodness and mercy shall follow me all the days of my life:
And I will dwell in the house of the LORD forever."

Afterwards we sit in a silent vigil. We're all pleading with God to show his favor on our dear friend and teammate…. #60.

Please God…save Sam…save Sam.

Sleep starts to weigh heavily on us and eventually we find spots on the floor or create makeshift beds out of chairs and couches out of sheer exhaustion.

Around 8:00 AM that morning we are awakened by one of the attending physicians. Dr. Miller is aware that a number of Sam's friends are waiting in the reception area and he gives an update on Sam's condition to Mr. and Mrs. Johnson who arrived a short while ago.

Dr. Miller takes the Johnsons aside and in a calm demeanor explains, "I want you to know that Sam is stable but his condition is very serious. Fortunately he regained consciousness last night shortly after he arrived. We performed emergency surgery to remove his spleen and stabilize multiple fractures of his left hip, arm and leg. Sam's left side took the full impact of the fall. Taking everything into consideration Sam is doing remarkably well. There appears to be no brain or spinal cord injuries. He's resting well but I must tell you that he will require a number of additional surgeries and lengthy rehabilitation just in the hopes of regaining some semblance of a normal gait. You can see him now, but Sam is heavily sedated so don't expect to talk long today."

After a short visit with Sam, Mr. Johnson relays the information on Sam's condition to folks in the waiting room. We breathe a collective sigh of relief that our prayers have been answered and Sam is alive and sometime in the future will be a student again. However, shortly after reality hits and we start to understand that no longer will the hard-nosed, right guard, #60 from Norwich be blocking opponents for the Mules. The team lost a piece of its core today, but it is essential we find the resolve to help Sam and ourselves move forward...one small step at a time.

When we are finally permitted to see Sam two days later, they grant our special request to have the entire team visit his room for a few minutes. We are led by the Coaches and next year's senior captain, Jon Lambert, our middle linebacker. Sam smiles as thirty-some guys invade his room, a line spilling out into the hallway.

With a big grin Coach Sam jokes, "Johnson, you really left a huge depression in the sidewalk when you hit it. You'll be getting a bill for the damage." Always the ballbuster, Coach broke the ice with his style of humor. His effort found the mark because a strained smile surfaces on Sam's face as he lays in bed.

"How are you feeling?" Coach Marino asks, shifting the conversation.

"Not too bad. They still have me on hefty painkillers, but I can't do anything with my left side since I broke just about every bone in my left leg, arm and hip," Sam utters in a shallow, pained voice.

Chet steps to the front of Sam's bed to offer his encouragement. "The Team wants you to know that we'll be dedicating next season to you. Number 60 will be worn on everybody's shoulder until you return to the field."

> *Our hearts were holding out for hope but our minds knew full well that Sam's football career was over.*

Captain Jon hands over a Muhlenberg game football to Sam with the entire team's signatures and proclaims, "This is just a down payment. When we win the MAC championship you will get another game ball. Everybody knows balls come in pairs." We smirk at the testicle reference, but deep down we recognize we've made a commitment that we need to deliver on for Sam and for ourselves.

We will regain Mule pride.

Chapter Five

"Tank gets a wet wake-up call"

It had been a few weeks since Sam's accident, and the entire campus was still in shock. His tragic fall made me forget temporarily about my J-Term trip to the Soviet Union. A group of thirty-three Muhlenberg students including myself were scheduled to spend the last three weeks of January studying abroad after Christmas break.

But our focus tonight is on Sam and a number of us decide to go to the Shanty for some beers and share "Sam stories". About eight of us with a few fake IDs pile into Tasmanian Devil's car and head for 19th Street. Tas is elected driver since he's on medication for some strange sounding virus and can't drink.

When we arrive at the bar, we are taken to a booth in the back with two large bench seats. Everybody is having a groovy time as the beer flows liberally. Tank is totally wasted and tries to hit on two girls at an adjacent table. They are townies and don't go to Muhlenberg.

"Ladies, do you like football?" Tank blurted out, bobbing his head slightly as he fights to exert control over his motor skills.

"It's okay," replied the closest girl, showing little interest in talking to a man that's been drinking solidly for three hours.

"Ah...my name is Terry and I play football for Muhlenberg College. What's your name?"

"Amanda, and this is my friend Danielle."

"I prefer Dani," said the other girl emphatically.

Tank's social awareness and powers of perception are depleted with each passing beer he inhales. At this moment he is incapable of reading facial expressions and seeing the girls aren't impressed with his "pigskin" exploits nor his brutish Jersey charm.

"Why don't you girls join us for a round so we can get to know each other," mutters Tank in slurred speech.

Amanda was quick to shoot down Tank's advance. "That's a nice offer but we just finished eating and have to go." Despite multiple pleas from Tank, the girls evacuate the Shanty post haste as if someone had pulled the fire alarm.

Tank is visibly pissed and blasts us for what he perceives as a lack of trying on our part. Stuttering and missing his words routinely Tank shouts, "Youuuu fuckheads are real pussies. All you want...to do is sit there and pound your parrots. You're real jive turkeys."

The Jet and I attempt to cheer Tank up by getting his mind off the bitchin' babes that just snubbed him. So we steer the conversation back to Sam and some of the crazy things he's done on and off the gridiron. After a few stories Tank gets increasingly emotional and yells to the Shanty patrons, "Sam is a gggreatttt guy! He's one of the toughest sons-of-bitches I've ever played with. I'm gonna shave number sixty on my back to honor him!"

This is a gesture Tank is well-equipped to do. He is one of the hairiest human beings God ever created. Any time Tank has his shirt off it looks like he's wearing a full black sweater. Small animals occasionally get lost in his back hair.

With Tank getting increasingly agitated, and not wanting to wrestle with a 265-lb. mental patient in the middle of the Shanty, we coax him to go home and make assurances that we'll assist with his commemorative request.

It was after midnight and we try to find a shaver that can cut through Tank's dense body hair. No one wants to use their personal electric shavers nor could a face shaver penetrate his abundant mane anyway. Lucky for us Robbie Boll, a wide receiver on the team, is watching TV at the Frat. Robbie lives just a few blocks off campus and likes to hang out with us.

He says, "My sister is a hair stylist and I think she has some clippers at home. I'll be back in less than fifteen minutes." We're all happy with that solution and encourage Boll to be quick. The Big Boy is getting restless.

A half hour later Robbie walks in the front door with hair clippers. At this point, Tank is virtually comatose and is lying face down on the floor of the living room sans shirt.

At least a dozen of us surround Tank laughing our asses off. Since I'm his roommate I have the honor of shaving a #60 on the wooly mammoth. Taking my time I methodically cut out the six and then the zero. It covers most of the shoulder blades.

It's a pretty good job if I must say so myself.

Ever the ballbuster, Wolfman grabs the shears and exclaims, "We can't pass up this opportunity." He begins to shave something else on Tank's lower back. After thirty seconds we make out a large penis and balls. At this point Tank is so out of it he doesn't realize what's going on. The rest of us are busting a gut laughing.

All we can do now is help Tank to his bed. We live on the second floor at the top of the front stairs. It's all we can do to drag him up while he attempts to climb the stairs on all fours. After much effort, we finally secure Tank in his bottom bunk bed. It's not hard to imagine why I picked the top bunk as soon as I saw the room layout. No way that 265-lbs of hairy, man meat is going to hang over my head every night. I can't trust the bed frame even if it is reinforced steel.

I'm so tired from getting Tank into bed that I forget I have not relieved myself all night. There are two factors that contributed to my current state. At the Shanty I was seated on the inside of the four-person bench, so going to the bathroom would have meant climbing over three guys to alleviate myself. Way too much inconvenience. Secondly, when I got to the frat house there was so much excitement around the Tank shearing celebration that the urge to pee was subdued.

It's now 2:30 AM and all I want to do is sleep. With my clothes on, I crawl onto the top bunk for a good night's sleep. Little do I realize that while I'm asleep, my kidneys are awake.

Sometime after 3:00 AM a freezing sensation overtakes me. As I lay shivering, still half-asleep I become vaguely aware that I'm resting in a pool of fluid. Too tired to investigate further at this late hour, I climb down from the top bunk and tumble onto our couch in the middle of the room. The rest of the night I sleep like a baby.

Sometime near noon I hear Tank cry out, "What the fuck?"

As I look over from the couch I begin to piece together the circumstances from last night's adventure. From what I see there is something like water dripping from the top mattress onto Tank's head. I connect that piece of information with the fact that my pants are soaking wet. It's at that very moment the convergence of details brings me to the conclusion that I pissed my bed last night and Tank is actually tasting my urine.

It didn't take Tank long after that to arrive at the same conclusion and yell, "Cornhole, you fucker! You...you pissed all over me!"

"Just to be clear I pissed on my bed and not you. If anything is to blame it is gravity along with a very porous mattress."

Not amused Tank makes a threatening move towards me and I run out of the room as fast as I can.

Tank shouts, "I will get you ...you motherfucker! And when I do I'm gonna put my foot up your ass!"

That proposition doesn't sound inviting, so I make a quick move for the door knowing that in an open field Tank is never going to catch me. Tank makes several attempts in vain to collar me but I don't fail to keep ten yards between us. Finally as the Big Man slows down to a walk I come up with a clever diversion tactic. Remind Tank what Wolfman did to him last night.

"Tank hold on. I need to tell you something as your friend and roommate. After I shaved Sam's number on your back..." Not letting me finish my sentence Tank interrupts, "You shaved my back?"

"You asked me to. Don't you remember? You love Sam. You wanted to honor Sam. You asked me to carve #60 on your back at the Shanty to honor him."

"I guess I do." says Tank.

"Like, get ready for this piece of news because I don't think you're gonna be very happy when you hear it," I cautiously inject.

"Not happy? How can I be madder than I am now? You peed on me!"

"Well Tank.....after I got done shearing a beautiful #60 on your back, Wolfman grabbed the clippers and cut out a penis and balls on you."

Tank yells out, "A penis! I am walking around with a dick on my back?"

"Yes, I'm afraid you are the proud owner of a wiener just above your ass crack. On the bright side, I don't think people interpreted anything from the two carvings like you want to do the nasty with Sam. And there were very few photos taken."

"Photos! There are photos?!?"

"Yeah, I think Wolfman snapped a few pics," I explain, trying my best to keep Tank calm.

Tank stomps off looking for Wolfman and my diversion works to perfection. Tank no longer is focused on the fact that my urine found its way into his mouth and is currently out to shower his wrath on Wolfman. Mission accomplished. In the days to come Tank will begrudgingly accept our apologies. Being a loyal roommate I agree to shave his entire back so he's no longer a poster boy for erotic art.

Chapter Six

"Commitment at Christmas"

A few days before Christmas, a number of us gather at the Palmisano's house in Whitehouse, NJ for a genuine Italian dinner. Mrs. P is a great cook and her lasagna is the stuff of culinary legends. Besides an opportunity to enjoy good food and company, we use this occasion to plot out our path to future football success.

With our bellies full, we lumber down to the basement where twenty of us cram around the television set to watch the AFC Divisional playoff game between the Pittsburgh Steelers and Oakland Raiders. It appears that the Raiders are going to win a 7-6 victory when a miracle happens.

With less than twelve seconds left in the game, Terry Bradshaw, the Steelers quarterback, under tremendous pressure from the Raider defensive line escapes two tackles and throws a pass to Frenchy Fugua. As the ball reaches Frenchy, there's a tremendous collision with Raiders safety Jack Tatum. The ball deflects backwards about ten yards and is headed for the ground when Pittsburgh running back Franco Harris catches the deflected ball just before it hits the ground and sprints 40 yards to the end zone for a touchdown and a 13 – 7 final score. Myron Cope, the Pittsburgh sportscaster dubs the catch "The Immaculate Reception".

The raucous crowd at Three Rivers Stadium in Pittsburgh, PA races out of the stands and mobs the field. Palmisano's basement is equally ecstatic.

"I don't believe it! It's a friggin' miracle!" screams Arnie.

"This is the Steelers first playoff win ever. It's incredible," says Tank.

Paul adds, "This is the type of mojo we need for the Mules."

Inspired by the Franco's miracle catch, I devise a plan to get our team prepared for next season.

"Guys, I've got an idea on what we should do this summer to get ready for the season. Let's rent a house at the Jersey Shore and do team workouts together there. What better way to condition than in the heat of the beach? We can run the sand dunes. What do you say?"

"That's a wicked rad idea," says Chet the Jet Stringer.

"And like, we can slip in a little partying while we're there...just for relaxation, ya know. Muscles gotta recover," adds Chuck Biers.

"My Uncle has a big rental house on LBI in Surf City. On 12th Street. It's four stories and can sleep a couple dozen people I think," says Robbie Boll. "It used to be an old boarding house that my Uncle Ed remodeled. If we all get jobs we can afford to rent it for the season."

Everyone agrees that renting a house together on LBI is a good idea. LBI stands for Long Beach Island, an 18-mile barrier island off the coast of New Jersey about 45 minutes north of Atlantic City. It's home to about 20,000 people year-round but swells to 100,000 during the summer months. LBI is a little slice of heaven with long stretches of sandy beaches, cute chicks and rowdy bars.

The challenge now is to find summer jobs on LBI and broaching the subject with my parents. When I'm about to start the conversation, Dad launches a pre-emptive strike about my semester grades. "I received your grades in the mail and I'm not impressed. Your GPA is under a 3.0."

"In fairness Dad, you're not seeing the improvement I've made from my mid-term grades. I raised up three of my five courses."

"Don't graduation honors start at 3.25?" he inquired.

I nodded and replied, "Yes, I've got a long way to go for cum laude but I've got something else to share. About twenty of us Muhlenberg football players want to live and train together as a team this summer. A central location is the Jersey Shore and we think the sand dunes and heat will be good for conditioning. We plan to work out in the morning before our shifts begin and again in the late afternoon."

"Do you have a place to live in mind?" says Mom in a concerned voice.

"Yeah, Robbie Boll's Uncle owns a big rental property on LBI that can handle twenty or more players and we think we may be able to get it," I answer.

"That's totally cool. I want to spend the summer there too!" exclaims my very excited sister who's in her senior year of high school.

"Judy, come on, it's an all-bros thing...just a dude ranch. There's no way you're staying in a house with twenty guys," I reply. I've always been protective of my sister. She's a pretty girl, even though I wouldn't admit it to her face. A number of my high school buddies try to ask her out and I routinely do my best to discourage any fraternization.

> *I only want the best for Judy and that's not living with twenty animals.*

"Judy, put any ideas of living at the Shore with the Muhlenberg football team out of your head," states Mom in a calm demeanor.

"Jack, you're gonna need a job if you plan to pull this off. I've got a business acquaintance, Brady Stuart, that may be able to help in that effort. He runs a miniature golf course around Surf City and is always looking for good help in the summer. I think the course is called The Sandbar," says Dad.

"That's perfect because no one plays miniature golf in the mornings. My hours will most likely be later in the day. Dad, can you talk to Mr. Stuart for me?" I ask.

"I'll make the introduction but you need to talk with Mr. Stuart yourself."

A week later my Dad arranges for me to talk with Mr. Stuart. Interestingly enough, Mr. Stuart's best time to talk with me is the morning of New Year's Eve. We talk for almost an hour and at the end of the interview he offers me a job for the summer. Mr. Stuart tells me the hours would rotate. Monday, Tuesday, and Wednesday I'd cover the hours of 10:00 AM to 5:00 PM, and on Fridays and Sundays I'd work 4:00 PM to 11:00 PM, actually closing the course sometimes. My hourly rate will be $2.20.

> *This is going to be good money, well above $1.60/hr minimum wage.*

Driving back home, I overhear news that dampens my enthusiasm with my new summer gig. Over the car radio comes breaking news that Roberto Clemente, one of the greatest baseball players of our generation, died in a plane crash off the coast of Puerto Rico. He was en route to deliver aid to Nicaraguan earthquake victims. The newscaster went on to say that the plane, a Douglas DC-7 was overloaded by 4,200 pounds. It crashed into the ocean after departing from San Juan Airport. He left behind his wife, Vera and three young sons, Roberto Jr., Luis Roberto, and Roberto Enrique.

What a day. I find a summer job but lose a childhood hero.

> *Roberto Clemente will never be forgotten as a ball player and a humanitarian.*

With my summer plans solidified, it's time to focus on getting ready for my January break—some international study and Soviet adventure.

Chapter Seven

"Bolshoi and Borscht"

We arrive in Moscow around 2:30 AM from Copenhagen on January 5th, arriving late due to airline delays. Five ATO brothers are among the thirty-plus students in this study exchange. Besides myself, in attendance are Burt Massa, Jim "Tas" Shapiro, Stan Painter and Rich Lapinski representing our fraternity.

We're transported to the Hotel National that's situated near Red Square. Between customs, baggage processing and transit challenges it takes us two hours to reach the hotel. Even though it's 4:30 in the morning, Jim and I can't sleep. We walk up to Red Square and are faced with a surreal experience. We stand in the middle of the square in awe of the Kremlin and St. Basil's Cathedral. It's just the two of us, two cleaning women and a boatload of KGB on guard.

At 5:00 AM we witness the changing of the guard at Lenin's Mausoleum. Unbelievable precision is executed by the soldiers in uniform. Waving eerily above the Kremlin is the red Soviet flag with the hammer and sickle.

"We're not in Kansas anymore, Toto."

Tensions between the Soviet Union and the US have run high since the 1962 Cuban Missile Crisis. Recently Leonid Brezhnev, the Soviet Leader fueled the fire when he challenged US foreign policy on a public broadcast:

"Of late, attempts have been made in the USA-at a high level and in a rather cynical form, to play the 'Chinese card' against the USSR. This is a shortsighted and dangerous policy."

Even on our short visit we sense the strained relationship as we are followed and monitored almost everywhere we go, presumably by the KGB.

The next morning Tas, my roommate, and I are surprised to learn that Russian hotels don't always have warm water. No matter how we position the showerhead the water temperature is frigid.

"Cobber, we gotta to psych each other up. We need a shower bad. We've been traveling for two days in the same duds. We gotta do this," Tas said.

Imitating a Marine drill sergeant, I slap Tas's face and shout in my loudest voice, "You sniveling coward. Take hold of your moldy ass and get in the shower soldier! No excuses shit bird!"

Tas disrobes and stands still in the stall while I turn on the shower. As the freezing cold water hits his body, he lets out a blood-curdling scream. "AHHHHHH SHIT FUCK!"

It's the quickest shower in the history of mankind. Tas doesn't even fully wash the soap out of his hair.

Now it's my turn. Tas reciprocates with an open hand smack to my face that he doesn't hold back on and imitates Coach Balls yelling, "Cobb, you piece of whale shit. You are the lowest of the low. You don't even deserve a shower. Get your ugly ass, poor excuse for a body in there and wash the stench from it. You're violating my nostrils!"

I too can't stop from involuntarily screaming as the icy blast hits my skin. "Ahhhh...this is fucked up! Those commie bastards are dicking with us!"

Hopefully the hotel staff didn't hear us.

This Russian water torture will end up repeating itself at numerous stops as we find the Soviet hot water delivery systems to be very unreliable. On this morning, after a quick breakfast of black bread and coffee, Tas and I walk up to see Red Square in the morning light.

The most impressive sight is the St. Basil's Cathedral with its collection of multi-colored, onion domes. We learn that Ivan the Terrible in the 16th century commanded the construction of the Cathedral and upon completion he had the architect's eyes poked out so that the designer would never again be able to build an equally beautiful structure anywhere else.

Now that's a screwed-up way to motivate future architects.

On top of that, it's essentially a miracle that St. Basil's is standing today. According to legend, Napoleon wanted it destroyed. His men lit fuses but they were supposedly snuffed by a sudden downpour.

This building is unbelievable. Glad it survived Napoleon and Stalin.

Our trip is arranged to not only include tours, but to also create opportunities to meet and speak with the Russian people. We're split into small groups with Russian counterparts that possess similar academic interests. Tas and I are studying the culture of sports within the Soviet Union. I'm intrigued how the Soviets test pre-teen children and channel them into specific sports academies if they demonstrate great potential. The Russian Sports Ministry creates essentially a factory system to develop young athletes at an early age. A much different approach than the US, where kids have their own free will usually try a variety of sports growing up and later specialize in one if they display the talent and choose to pursue it.

Being economics majors, Burt and I enter into a lot of discussions with Russian students regarding the Soviet economy and their 5-year plans. We repeatedly point out quality issues they're experiencing with their products and services as well as the lack of incentive in their system to innovate and improve things. But the most frustrating conversations focus on the aspect of freedom. Typical is the chat between Chris Ford, fellow student at Muhlenberg and Galina, a student at Moscow University.

"Does it bother you that you don't have total freedom in the Soviet Union?" Chris asks.

"We are free," Galina replies.

"But Galina, the government censors what you can read and listen to. You cannot read certain books." Chris explains.

"But we are free," Galina again replies.

"You also can't travel from city to city without permission from the government." Chris says.

"But we are free to move around," Galina responds stoically.

The circular conversations seem to go nowhere. I guess if you've never experienced real freedom, you don't truly understand it. It's like if you have never eaten ice cream, you don't miss the taste of it.

Our next stop is the City of Riga in the Republic of Latvia. Riga is an important seaport and industrial hub in the Baltic Sea region. While it's considered part of the Soviet Union, Latvia is a stark contrast to Russia. You notice it as soon as you walk down the streets. Latvians wear significantly more colorful, stylish dress than the bleak individuals we observed in Moscow. Latvians also smile much more than the somber demeanor of Muscovites. We learn that it's actually an insult to be called a Russian if you are Latvian because of prior political conflicts with Russia.

The first night we meet a friend of Chris's named Irina who attends the University of Riga. Apparently they developed a relationship through letters via Chris's Russian Studies class. Tas, Rich, Chris, Irina and I go into town and enjoy a local rock band. We drink, dance and talk the night away.

The night is significant because it's the beginning of a long-term relationship between Tas and Chris. I've never seen Tas so concerned about impressing a girl before. But each morning of the trip he makes me look him over for a grooming and dress inspection. I help him the best I can.

From a physical perspective they're opposites. Tas is a dark-skinned, 5'5", stocky wrestler, while Chrissie is a 5'9" slender beauty with a fair complexion. While they have this Beauty and the Beast thing going on, it doesn't matter. They enjoy each other's company and complement each other's sense of humor.

I'm overjoyed to be an eyewitness to their budding relationship. Happy for Tas.

The great thing about the trip format is that only half of our time is scheduled with conferences, tours, lectures, etc., and the rest of the time is unscheduled for meeting people informally and working on our projects.

One of those unscheduled events unfolded when we attended a Church service Sunday morning. We meet Matolis, the only Arch Bishop in the Communist world. Virtually his entire congregation is comprised of a few, older, peasant-looking individuals. The low attendance is no doubt directly attributable to the government's opposition to religion.

Later that day Chris takes us to the apartment of a relative, her mother's cousin. What strikes me is how little living space there is for a family of seven. It's a tiny 80-square meter flat that consists of a couple of rooms with a kitchen and bathroom. The space is overrun with books and paintings. The head of the family is the Chief Professor of Architecture at the Polytechnic Institute and he earns a mere 320 rubles a month (around $10 USD). In the US he'd most likely be living in a large, single family home, but the Soviet system doesn't allow for that. He is allotted limited space in a government-owned building based upon his position and the number of people living with him.

After a week in Latvia, we travel back to Moscow. The food throughout the trip is pretty funkadelic but some of the items I don't dig. One of those is borscht, a soup made from beetroot, cabbage and potatoes. It's a staple of their diet, but when it's a lunch option I resort to stuffing myself with black bread.

The subway system in Moscow is very impressive. The cars are clean and the tunnels are decorated with attractive murals. One afternoon, Tas and I start randomly riding the subway to various stations to experience areas outside the city. It's not uncommon to see significant poverty once you leave Moscow proper. We try to take photos of the impoverished areas, but that's when it becomes apparent that we're being followed. When we attempted to take our cameras out, two men dressed in suits leapt from out of nowhere to strongly discourage our photo-journalistic efforts.

To test the theory we are being followed, I whisper to Tas,"Start walking slowly down the street. When we get to the intersection up ahead let's take a hard left and run down that road to see if these guys follow us."

It took us a few minutes to slowly walk to the intersection, and once there we made a sharp left turn and ran as fast as we could for a few blocks like a junkyard dog was chasing us. We dove into an alley and used that as our observation point. Sure enough, as we looked out from the narrow passageway we saw the two men running to look for us. Once we were in their sights they gave us stern, disapproving looks but say nothing.

Later that day after another stop on the subway we're convinced we see Aleksandr Solzhenitsyn, the famous Russian author. We had to read his book, "One Day in the Life of Ivan Denisovich" in Russian Literature class. In fact it is that professor, Dr. Ziedonas that's our host and organizer for the trip. Solzhenitsyn is not popular with the Soviet government because he's an unrelenting critic of Communist totalitarianism and speaks out against the Soviet Union's forced labor camps that he's experienced firsthand.

The old dude we spy at a distance possesses a distinctive long beard and disheveled, receding hairline like Solzhenitsyn. However we soon discover many older, Russian men are digging that scene. In all probability there's no way the guy we're watching is Solzhenitsyn since he's most likely in a Soviet prison at this very moment. However that doesn't stop Tas and I from regaling our travel partners with stories of our clandestine meeting with the famous Russian dissident later that evening.

The highlight of our visit is the trip to the Bolshoi Ballet. One glance at the Bolshoi Theatre's iconic façade, with its sculpture of a Roman Chariot drawn by four rearing horses above the white pillared roof, and we know we're somewhere very special. The extraordinary ambience continues on the inside with a plush, elegant interior that includes five balcony levels with gold-leaf trim. The company is performing Sleeping Beauty. While we sit up in the nose-bleed section, we're trippin on the performance big-time. The precision and athleticism of the dancers is a total stone-cold groove.

Upon conclusion of the ballet, there are seven curtain calls and standing ovations. Somewhere between the fifth and sixth curtain calls, Tas and I make our way down from our balcony seats and we stand in the aisle directly in front of the stage. We're in total awe of featured dancers that just performed the lead roles. The two sculpted athletes take their final bows. The female dancer curtsies methodically with no facial expressions or eye contact and never acknowledges the cheering throng of admirers. Her stoic body language says, "Look at me, love me, but keep your distance you insignificant peons."

In stark contrast the personable male lead gazes directly down on us and smiles as he hails the adoration of the crowd. His body language conveys, "Hey I'm glad you enjoyed the show and let's face it....wasn't I the best thing in it?"

There were no words to express the awe-inspiring feeling we experience at this moment.

From Moscow we travel to Leningrad where I spent the afternoon at a boarding school that hosts promising athletes. They receive comprehensive coaching and training for their particular sport. We also visit the nearby Physical Culture Institute, a college where approximately 1500 students prepare to be coaches and Olympic hopefuls. We meet a female Russian shot put champion who's studying there. Her name is Olga and she's very proud of the fact she's throwing the shot put nine feet further than any of our US women. A fact she repeats more than once. Despite her ample ego, she'd make an ass-kicking defensive tackle for the Mules. Olga could be our "Russian Nightmare" as she disembowels helpless running backs attempting to gain yardage on us.

All in all, the Soviet trip represents a way-cool cultural experience, and it solidifies my feeling that with all our imperfections, the United States rocks. Our political and economic systems aren't perfect, but they're totally rad when compared to any other country in the world.

The trip also brought together two very special people, Chrissie and Tas, into a lasting relationship. Not a bad J-term at all.

Chapter Eight   "Twenty-one gun salute"

The January break is fun, but it feels good to return to school and get back in a routine. Most of the football players are getting in at least four off-season conditioning workouts a week.

Today is Scott Cressman's birthday. Prize Hog is turning twenty-one and we've got a special way to celebrate his reaching this important milestone that he'll experience later this evening. It's late afternoon and Scott, Jim Shapiro, Chris Duffler and I are laying around Benfer Hall shooting the breeze. Being economics and business majors, we're speculating on entrepreneurial efforts that we could do on campus to make money.

"With all the horny, lonely dudes we have here at 'Berg we could make a killing with an escort service or a room-service brothel," says Chris.

I nod in agreement and reply, "Chris, you're right. Let's create a business plan. Our operating margins will be dynamite!"

"We don't need a large investment to start with because we can have the girls go directly to the guys rooms," counters Jim. "We just need a couple of motivated, cooperative young ladies."

"Wel-l-l-l-l...you guys are big talkers. You're trippin' over your tongues, you bogus butt humps. You three would pee your tighty-whitees if you even saw a hooker cross the street," says a cynical Scott.

"Dream on Big Man. If you think we're bluffing here's the skinny. We'll bring back a lady of the evening to your crib by nine o'clock or we'll give you fifty bucks. But if we bring the goods you owe us fifty smackers," I reply.

"You got a bet Cobber. I'm gonna love taking your dough...you pussies," cracked Scott.

I replied, "You just be hanging around tonight for your bodacious babe and have the money with you big boy."

Jim doesn't want any part of the bet, but Chris and I don't dig our manhood being challenged and shake Scott's hand without hesitation. We quickly went off to make a plan.

"Our best shot, Chris, is to boogey down to Hamilton Street. There's a bar there, The Shadowbox, that sits next to a strip club. Hookers must hang near there," I explain.

"The Shadowbox...isn't that the dive where a guy was shot last week?!" Chris replied.

"Duffler, take a chill pill. Don't be buggin' out. We can pull this off. Do you still have that brown overcoat?" I ask.

"Yeah but what's so righteous about the overcoat?" asks Chris.

I reply, "Listen, we need to look bad-ass. You're six-foot-four but weigh a hundred and sixty pounds...but when you put on the overcoat you look like a fucking gangster. It hides your skinny frame. We don't want people jacking us around."

So the two of us head down to the Shadowbox with our overcoats and best "mafia form". Chris even brought a cane that made him appear more threatening.

Nice touch, Chris.

We park the car and head for the bar. It's dimly lit and looks like an old railroad depot. The bouncer, a very large black man, weighing about three hundred pounds sits on a stool and nods at us to go in. As we brush past, I notice he had a little smile on his face. I'm sure he knows we're jive honkeys who are full of shit and have no place being there, but his curiosity gets the best of him and he feels charitable.

Once in the door both Chris and I are confronted with the reality that this is predominately a black bar. We stick out like sore thumbs. Blaring over the DJ's system is the song, Back Stabbers by the O'Jays:

> (What they do!)
> (They smile in your face)
> All the time they want to take your place
> The back stabbers (back stabbers)
> (They smile in your face)
> All the time they want to take your place
> The back stabbers (back stabbers)

Feeling a bit uneasy, we quickly order two beers and down them as fast as we can. Ten minutes later, we stood outside the bar.

"Chris, this a real bummer. We can't go back to Scott empty-handed. We've got to do something," I said.

Chris replies, "I hear ya but I ain't going back in the Shadowbox. We're lucky we didn't get our asses kicked."

"Wait, take a gander down the street. Our luck may be changing. Is that a hooker?" I say.

One block over is a five-foot-five, black woman in a super-short, purple mini-dress that barely covers two-thirds of her ample caboose. She appears a little tipsy in her black platform heels as she heads right for us.

"Hey white boys, you be looking for a good time?" asks the young lady.

Trying to remain as cool as I can I nervously utter, "Hey gir-l-l-l, what's up? What's your handle?" I ask.

"Sapphire," replies our new acquaintance.

Following up I make a proposal, "Sapphire, we'd like to hire your services, but not for us. We go to Muhlenberg College and we've got a buddy there in dire need of pootie tang."

"No way! Ya'all crazy. I know dat trick. You be scamming me, Don't jive me, white boys. You get me to the crib and then its gang-bang time," says a reluctant Sapphire.

"No way. You've gotta trust us. On my Mama's grave, it's just one guy, but he's a big dude...over six-feet and about two-hundred and thirty pounds," I add.

"That's gonna cost you," replies Sapphire.

We agree on a price of forty dollars. That's cool with us because we will still net out ten bucks profit after Scott pays off the bet and we salvage our reputations as "can-do business men". Throughout the ten-minute drive back to the college we reassure Sapphire that we're legit and not up to something. We're lucky that Sapphire is probably the only prostitute in Allentown without a pimp because no way a pimp would let us drive off with one of his girls unless we leave Chris for collateral and that wasn't going to happen.

We park at Benfer Hall around 8:15 and climb the stairs to the second floor leading to Scott's room. His dorm layout consists of four, two-person rooms surrounding a living room with an adjacent bathroom. As we saunter through the front door of Scott's suite accompanied by Sapphire we see Scotty stretched out on the living room couch. Chris and I are sporting cheek-to-cheek grins like two Cheshire cats that just ate a flock of canaries. The startled look on Scott's face is totally awesome. Most of the color has drained from his head...maybe both heads.

"What's hanging, Big Man? This is Sapphire and she's here to make your dreams come true!" I announce with great pride.

"Ahhhh no way," cries Scott.

"Way," I reply.

Sapphire proceeds to lead my Prize Pig to slaughter as she takes his hand and guides him to the nearest bedroom. The door shuts and the living room breaks out in spontaneous laughter.

We can't hear anything except a radio playing Elton John's "Rocket Man".

Somebody's rocket is gonna go off...let's hope not prematurely.

I'm convinced that Scott is just talking with Sapphire because he's too scared to do anything. They emerge from the bedroom about 20 minutes later and Scott does his best to convince us that he's God's gift to love-making. Sapphire plays along with the charade to make Scott feel like a stud.

Chris and I drive Sapphire back downtown and pay her the forty bucks we promised.

"Nice doing business witchu boys. Cum again sometime," Sapphire says with a big smile.

"Right on Sapph. You were totally cool tonight. Props for helping the Big Man learn about the facts of life. Catch you on the flip side," I reply.

When we get back to campus Chris and I go straight to Benfer Hall to do a little more gloating with Scott and to make sure we get our money. Without hesitation Scott hands over the fifty bucks. While we made ten bucks from the adventure, our entrepreneurial enthusiasm to establish a room service brothel on campus leaves us for good. This really isn't the gig for us.

Feeling the need to celebrate Scott's special day I say, "Let's go over to ATO. Our brothers have a keg waiting for you in honor of your birthday and we also have to do our salute."

"Alright let's do this thing, ya know,"replies Scott.

For the next couple hours we party hard and finish off the keg. Right around midnight I let the guys know it's time for our "twenty-one gun salute" to Scott. What that means is lining Chew Street, the road right out in front of the frat, with at least twenty-one guys and removing our pants. For the salute to be official it has to be frontal nudity and not mooning. While ATO is smack dab in the middle of a residential area the neighbors are pretty tolerant of our shenanigans as long as we expose ourselves late in the evenings when the little kids are asleep.

So here we are. About twenty-five dudes on both sides of Chew Street under the street lights nonchalantly with our pants down and our wankers out. We set a goal that we stay in formation until five cars pass us. The last car was the best. The driver is a nice little old lady approximately seventy-five years-old just honking her horn with a big smile on her face while she gives us the thumbs-up sign.

It's a birthday Big Scott will never forget and for all we know it might be the first time he's experienced the touch of a woman. I'm just pleased that I could contribute to his personal growth and development.

You da man, Scott.

Chapter Nine

"Love blossoms in the Castle"

One of the first things I do when I return to campus after J-term is to check in on Debbie D'Angelo. The good news is that she's fully recovered from her bout with mono. It's time to accelerate my efforts to make her mine and separate her from her hometown honey. I need to figure out something big that would impress her. In my mind, I speculate over multiple dating scenarios. Finally I overhear one of the senior frat officers, Steiny talk about a restaurant in Reading, PA that is a castle.

Wow, what better way to impress Debbie than with a castle!

Steiny gives me all the details. The name of the restaurant is Stokesay Castle about forty miles from Allentown. He tells me I'd need to make a reservation well in advance and bring plenty of money. A sport coat is also required attire for men in the main hall.

My plan is to invite Debbie to dinner but I need another couple. It's always better karma to play off another couple. It keeps the conversation from dying.

One of the funniest couples around is the Wolfman and his longtime girlfriend, Gigi Garifino. I'll invite them.

Gigi is a pretty, petite blond with an enormous personality. Proud of her Italian heritage, Gigi has the ability to bust balls with the best of us. Her rapier wit and lightning-quick responses can put you on your heels before you open your mouth. Being able to go toe-to-toe with Greg on barbs is not easy for anyone, but Gigi does it with ease—always ending up with the last word.

Greg and I decide to combine a musical that's playing on campus, Fiorello, with dinner at Stokesay Castle to make it a special date. With the plans set, I ask Debbie and she says yes. Better yet, I'm receiving vibes from her that she may be beginning to like me more than just a casual friend. With everything moving along in good fashion, the only thing that worries me now is what if Gigi starts busting Debbie too much during the date. Debbie is much more reserved and might be overwhelmed with Gigi's machine-gun tongue.

I make sure that I pick up Greg and Gigi before Debbie so I can plead with them to go easy on her. As they jump in my '60 Caddy I greet them enthusiastically, "Hey guys. What's shaking?"

Greg takes one look at me in my checkered sports coat and multi-colored tie (handed down from Dad) and with his best Freddie Prinze impression says, "Looo-king Gooooood, Cobber!" Prinze is the lead actor for one of the most popular TV shows, Chico and the Man, and that's his signature line.

"Gigi, I've got a favor to ask of you tonight. This is my first real date with Debbie and I want it to go well. She seems to be a bit shy so can you please go easy on her tonight?" I ask with anxious optimism.

"Cobber, if brains were taxed, you'd get a rebate. I don't intend to engage in a battle of wits with you or Debbie, because I don't fight with unarmed persons." Gigi jokes.

"That's exactly what I am talking about. Can you just go slow with Debbie?" I ask again.

"Just chill Cobberino. I'll be cool. You're a good person with an open mind. I can feel the breeze from here…no really, I'm just having some fun with you." Gigi adds.

After picking up Debbie, we head to the school auditorium to see Fiorello. It's a musical about New York City Mayor, Fiorello LaGuardia. We all enjoy the show but best of all it keeps Gigi quiet for two hours.

As soon as the curtain drops to end the play, I drive to the restaurant to make a 9:00 dinner reservation. While Gigi is somewhat restrained in the car ride, she still manages to insult my checkered sport coat when she says, "Hey Cobber, what pimp did you steal the coat from?"

The restaurant is more impressive than I imagine. Modelled after the original thirteenth century Stokesay Castle in Shropshire, England, it's a massive stone structure with an authentic, medieval interior. The main dining room boasts an ornate wood fireplace highlighted by gargoyle carvings. Huge wooden beams frame the cathedral ceiling from which hang two candle chandeliers. The four of us are escorted to our table and settle into plush, oversized upholstered chairs.

As far as I'm concerned, the evening is a rousing success. All four of us enjoy the Castle and Debbie seems to be impressed with my efforts. As it turns out Debbie is easy to talk to and Gigi didn't verbally rip my date to shreds. Although she did ask a number of questions about Debbie's Modern Dance Team and their provocative outfits. I was a little nervous with where Gigi was going with that line of questioning but it stopped with her saying, "Cobber loves skimpy outfits, don't you big guy."

After I drop off Greg and Gigi, I walk Debbie to her dorm room. A cool breeze makes it a bit chilly and I wrap my pimpesque sport coat around her shoulders. During the ten-minute stroll back to Debbie's dorm, I take the opportunity to ask her to Founders Day Weekend. Annually this three-day celebration honors the founding fathers of ATO and represents the biggest social event of the year for the frat. The weekend of fun typically begins on a Friday with a sit-down formal dinner at the frat house, followed by a kick-ass party on Saturday night and finishes with a clam bake on our patio Sunday afternoon.

With Founders Day weekend still two months away, I'm confident that Debbie's calendar should be open. I soon discover that's not the case.

"Jack, I'm sorry but I have tickets with my sister to see Billy Joel at Princeton University that Saturday night," Debbie said.

"Well can you go to the dinner and the clam bake on Friday and Sunday?" I ask.

"I'd love to," replies Debbie.

"That's awesome. It should be a funkadelic time," I declare.

As we get to the front door of Debbie's suite, I lean into her slowly for a kiss goodbye and to my pleasant surprise she digs it. In fact she places her arms around my waist to draw me closer. I sense that the hold of her hometown boyfriend is loosening as the kiss lingers on.

Even though the date's a success, I know I've got to overcome potential objections from Debbie's older sister, Jennifer D'Angelo, who is a junior at Muhlenberg. Jennifer is a model student, very conservative and from what I could tell extremely straight-laced. Jennifer somehow got the impression that I'm a party-guy who dates a lot of girls and drinks too much.

From my perspective I'm honing my social skills, friendly with a lot of people, many of whom happen to be of the opposite sex and I'm experimenting with various aspects of college life as any good, inquisitive student of life should do.

What aids my cause more than anything is that Debbie has a mind of her own and can be stubborn on certain issues. I actually believe that Jennifer's objections might help push Debbie in my direction. Whatever the dynamic, I feel the two of us getting more emotionally attached and I like it. I do understand Jennifer's apprehension. She's just doing what she thinks is best to protect her younger sister.

Chapter Ten

"There is tough and then there is Gable"

It's middle of March and the wrestlers at the frat; Jim Shapiro (Tasmanian Devil), Greg Wolfe (Wolfman) and Steve Holland (Preacher) present the football players with a unique opportunity. It's a chance to meet and hear Dan Gable conduct a wrestling clinic that's being held at nearby Lehigh University. Dan Gable is regarded as the greatest wrestler walking the face of the earth. He is the reigning 149-pound Olympic champion, having won the gold medal last August. But that simple statement of achievement doesn't do justice to his level of dominance over the sport. Prior to the 1972 Olympics, Dan competed in the most prestigious wrestling tournament in Russia, the Tbilisi Meet. He went through several Soviets on his way to being named the outstanding wrestler of the championships. Dan's achievement on Russian soil so angered the Soviet National Coach that he vowed, "Before the '72 Olympics, we will find someone to beat Gable."

Despite the fact that Dan severely injured his knee before the Olympics, he wrestled in the West Germany, Munich Games and performed the amazing feat of winning six matches without yielding a point to any of his opponents and pinning three of them en route to the gold medal. Not only did the Soviets fail in their quest to derail Dan, but the rest of the world did so as well and he wrestled basically on one leg.

But my wrestling buddies said there is more to the story than just Dan's Olympic experience and that he's an outstanding motivational speaker. They say the clinic is scheduled for this Sunday, targeting high school and college wrestlers. It's a one-day event with a clinic in the afternoon capped by a dinner in the evening with Gable as the guest speaker. Many of us football players had wrestled in high school and are open to attending the clinic.

> *Hopefully we can pair up with each other during the drills so we don't look foolish.*

As the day arrives for the clinic, about twenty of us drive down to Lehigh University in Bethlehem, PA along with our three Mule wrestlers. Only about a 15 minute drive from the 'Berg, Lehigh is known for its College of Engineering. As we enter the wrestling venue, Grace Hall (affectionately known as the Snake Pit), I'm struck by two things immediately. One, the place is packed with avid college wrestlers from all over: Penn State, Slippery Rock, Rutgers, Cornell, Hofstra, Edinboro, and the Minnesota Golden Gophers. Secondly, this building is steeped in tradition. Hanging on the walls are photos and plaques of their national champions and their team successes at national and EIWA championships. The entire atmosphere is intimidating for those of us that have not wrestled in years.

I quickly pair off with Chuck Biers, my fellow guard, who's similar in size and wrestling experience so we can go through the drills without being totally embarrassed by the real wrestlers.

Gable moves to the front of the mats with a wrestling partner that accompanies Dan to demonstrate the moves he is teaching the group. You could literally hear a pin drop as he begins to address us. Standing about five-feet, ten-inches and weighing probably around one-hundred and fifty pounds of ripped muscle, Dan has total command of this stage. You immediately sense his intensity and focus. He is a no-nonsense guy when it comes to training.

Throughout the day he literally beats the shit out of his designated partner as he demonstrates each move about five times before we are commanded to emulate the movement. I feel sorry for Dan's workout companion, because Dan is constantly reinforcing his philosophy of always being on the attack. It's not good enough to just secure a takedown on your opponent. According to Dan you have to take him down with the thought of putting him on his back with continuous aggression. It's just as much exercising mental discipline as it is a physical drill. Dan wants all of us to think multiple moves ahead and always with the thought of planting your adversary on his back.

Chuck and I look awkward compared to many of the other attendees, but we do get a lot out of the day's activities. The focus on balance and leverage will serve us well in the upcoming football season—but the greater reason for coming to the clinic is to hear Gable's motivational talk.

After we shower up, we are treated to a no frills chicken dinner. As the dessert is being served, Dan walks slowly up to the podium. What follows next is the greatest motivational talk I've ever experienced firsthand. He speaks of his early beginnings in high school and the terrible tragedy of losing his older sister, Diane. She was savagely murdered by a sixteen year-old boy who lived two blocks from the Gables. What made it more chilling was that Dan had a premonition of who did it even before the police told the family. He had a bad feeling about the neighbor boy who was making crazy remarks the week before. Dan spoke about the flurry of thoughts that entered his mind when police confirmed the murderer.

> *Maybe if I'd said something earlier, I could have saved her.*

> *Maybe if I had been home instead of on vacation with the family, I could have saved her.*

Somewhere Dan found the strength to help himself and his parents move forward after this unthinkable act of violence. Dan actually moved into Diane's room and focused his wrestling to honor her memory. Dan never lost a match in high school or college until his senior year. He entered his 1970, NCAA championship bout against Larry Owings from the University of Washington with a combined record of 181 wins and zero losses. One hundred and eighteen of those victories were at the college level representing Iowa State University, one of the perennial wrestling powers in the country.

What followed next was another turning point in his life. Admittedly he got caught up in the hype of finishing his college career undefeated with three straight NCAA championships. Dan lost focus at the worst possible time. In an epic battle he succumbed to Larry Owings by a score of 13 to 11. He used that bitter disappointment to rededicate himself to his sport and the rest is legendary. Dan Gable became the most dominant wrestler on the international scene as he won World and Olympic Championships.

We all had goose bumps listening to Dan and we swore to each other that we would remember Dan's motivational words when things got tough for us. Whether it be in two-a-day drills in the heat of August or in the fourth quarter of a game when our tongues were hanging out, we weren't going to back down from a challenge. Regardless, you ain't seen tough until you've met Dan Gable.

Chapter Eleven

"Founders Day Three-way"

It's early April, and Founders Day weekend is finally upon us. I'm excited that I'll get to spend two-thirds of it with my budding girlfriend, Debbie. The one loose end is my on-again, off-again relationship with my hometown girlfriend, Casey Erickson. Casey was a year behind me in high school and we went together my senior year. When she prepared to be a member of the first female class at Rutgers University, Casey let me know that she could not be tied down. The news hit me pretty hard as I completed my freshman year at Muhlenberg. She informed me last summer and my initial reaction was admittedly immature. I ripped out all references and photos of her in my high school yearbook. That was no small feat since she had pasted several tiny photos of herself all through my senior yearbook.

Secondly I did not go home for two days, sleeping at a local hospital where my buddy, Paul Palmisano was working as a summer security guard. That didn't sit well with my father. When I finally made it back to my parents' house that third night, Dad was waiting for me at the door.

"Do you know that your mother and I have been worried sick about you? We have not seen or heard from you in two days."

I responded sheepishly with, "I stayed with Paul Palmisano the last couple nights."

"I don't give a crap if you stayed with President Nixon. If you want to continue to live under my roof and have me pay your tuition you'll give your mother and I the common courtesy of a call. And before you sleep over anywhere you will get our permission. Is that clear?"

"Clear" I said. But I was hurting..."

Not letting me finish Dad said, "I don't want to hear it. There's no excuse. You will live by our rules or you can live on your own."

Even though I wanted to protest and try to make him understand my point of view, I knew I couldn't afford my own digs. So I sucked up my pride and apologized.

"Dad, I'm sorry. It won't happen again. I guess it was a case of temporary insanity." I said displaying as much remorse as I could muster.

"Okay Jack. Let's move on."

> *And despite my screwed-up sense of macho pride I knew he was right.*

Once Casey got through her first semester at Rutgers we started dating casually again. Since Debbie couldn't go with me to the Saturday night party, I thought I would ask Casey to go as friends.

The Founders Day formal dinner turns out to be a stone groove. Our cook, Busy Bob outdid himself with surf and turf—lobster and filet mignon. Dressed in a full-length, emerald green dress, Ms. D'Angelo is hotter than the Devil's butt. Seated with us are Wolfman and Gigi, living up to their reputations keeping the table banter lively.

This time around, Debbie is comfortable enough with the dynamic duo to produce some jabs herself.

The next day, Debbie is off to see Billy Joel at Princeton University. I sweated out coordinating the timing of Debbie's departure and Casey's arrival, but everything seems to be working out as planned. Debbie leaves just before noon and Casey arrives at the frat house around 4:00 PM. But when my frat brothers see Casey hanging with me at the house instead of Debbie, they can't wait to do a little ball-busting innuendo.

"Ohhh hey Casey and Cobber." Wolf-man says.

"What's happening?" Casey and I reply in unison.

"Casey, we missed you last night at the dinner," remarks Wolfman smugly.

Before Casey could answer, I interrupt and try to divert the conversation. "Casey was busy last night. Who's playing at the party tonight?"

"Wellll, I think the band's name is The Funky Threesome," jokes Greg.

"Really? That's stellar. I think they played at Moravian last week," I reply trying to keep my composure and not give in to Greg's veiled mocking.

"Hey Cobber. I'm studying different religions in my World Religion class. Aren't you a practicing Mormon?" I could use your help understanding their beliefs," Greg teased. Clearly in reference to the practice of polygamy.

"No I'm Lutheran but I have relatives who are Mormons. Maybe that's what you are thinking." I say.

"Ohhh okay," replies Greg. And after a short pause he continues his line of insinuation, "Man, I just checked out the flick, The Way We Were, pretty groovy. Robert Redford marries Barbara Streisand and then has an affair with his college girlfriend. Quite a hot triad."

At that moment I had to get Casey away from Greg for my own good. I say, "Yeah it was a sad deal. Hey, Casey and I gotta run. We're gonna grab some chow before the party."

"That sounds wicked good. My gut's growling. Can I hitch my wagon to you?" Greg asks.

"Ahhh, Casey and I need some alone time. Get my drift?" I reply.

"No sweat, Sherlock. See ya around." Greg replied. With that, I hustle Casey out of the room before she starts to piece together Wolfman's ramblings.

Later the party is in full gear when we return from chowing down. Our frat house is wall-to-wall peeps grooving on the band and our featured drink, "Purple Passion"—a grape-flavored grain alcohol concoction we make in an old-fashioned tub. It's a particularly lethal beverage because it tastes like grape juice but the alcohol content is 190-proof. Quite a kick.

Casey and I are sitting on a couch in the back of the living room. I'm not feeling particularly festive, especially since my thoughts continue to drift elsewhere. Casey sensing something isn't right and looks me straight in the eye and asks, "I can tell your head is somewhere else. Is there another person? You can tell me. Just be honest."

At that moment my emotions take over and I reply, "Yeah, I've been seeing someone here at Muhlenberg for a couple of months. Her name is Debbie." After an uncomfortable silence I continue, "I'm sorry I haven't said anything until now, but I wasn't sure where we were going."

"That's cool, Jack. We've been moving apart for some time now. Let's just have a nice evening and we'll go our separate ways tomorrow." Casey says.

I can't believe how extremely calm and under control Casey is. She's always been more mature than me throughout high school. In the morning, Casey takes off early and we never go out again.

Sunday morning brings abundant sunshine and blue skies. It's a perfect backdrop to initiate my plan to surprise Debbie with my frat pin and ask her to go steady at the clam bake. It's now 12:30 PM and over sixty frat brothers and guests are hanging out on our wrap-around stone patio. We wash down steamers, lobsters, corn on the cob and potatoes with a couple kegs of beer. After about an hour, I give a nod to Wolfman to alert the rest of the guys it was zero hour.

Jim Croce's "Time in a Bottle" is playing out of Burt Massa's second floor stereo speakers.

> "If I could save time in a bottle
> The first thing that I'd like to do
> Is to save every day 'til eternity passes away
> Just to spend them with you

If I could make days last forever
If words could make wishes come true
I'd save every day like a treasure and then
Again, I would spend them with you"

"Debbie, I've got something to ask you," I say.

"What is it Jack?" Debbie replies.

I slip my hand into my pocket and pull out my ATO pin. It's black onyx with gold Greek letters surrounded by twelve tiny opals. As I open the case, I press it into her hands and slowly say, "I'd like you to have my pin."

Debbie smiled with a look of surprise and asks, "Does this mean we're going together?"

"That's what I am trying to say. Well...?"

"Yes, I accept," replies Debbie.

At that moment all my ATO brothers gather around and began to serenade Debbie with our traditional song, The Sweetheart of ATO.

"Most girls I've met I'll soon forget,
They could never be true
'Cause for me there is only one
Who could stand for the Gold and Blue.

In my heart is a girl with a smile on her lips
Lovely to see, precious to me
With her eyes like the stars
And our rose in her hair
No one can quite compare.
When shadows try to hide us
Dreams will see us through

Tho the years come and go,
She'll be loyal I know,
She's the sweetheart of A T O."

Taken back by the public demonstration Debbie buries her head in my left shoulder as my brothers offer their congratulations. With our new arrangement, her hometown honey is now history and I couldn't be happier.

Chapter Twelve   "Life's a pisser"

The semester is coming to a close and most of us can't wait for our Jersey Shore summer to begin. Only two weeks of final exams and finishing term papers sit between us and our summer sabbatical of sunshine.

Throughout the spring, a number of us join the Allentown Rugby Club to see what that sport is all about. At first glance it seems like a natural extension of American football since the object of the contest is to advance a "puffed-up football" over a goal line to score or kick it through goal posts for a field goal. That's where the similarities end. Rugby, played with fifteen players instead of eleven is a much different game because there's no protective equipment and the methods of tackling we're taught in football are not practical in rugby. I learn that lesson the hard way when in my first contest against the Penn State Club Team I'm knocked out cold for about thirty-seconds as I tried to tackle a guy head on that outweighed me by fifty pounds. I recovered and eventually continued to play but my hard knocks education would not be forgotten.

A unique sight in rugby is the scrum. It looks like a group of men with their heads down pushing in a circle giving the appearance of hogs rooting in the dirt at dinnertime. A scrum takes place when two sets of forwards mass together around the ball and struggle to gain possession of the ball. Scrums are used to restart play after a violation occurs.

A great tradition associated with the sport of rugby is after a match both teams go out to a bar together for beer and song. No matter how heated the competition, both sides put aside the outcome and enjoy camaraderie and suds among combatants.

A crazy incident occurs today, but it's not associated with the rugby match. It's an extracurricular challenge that starts as a joke. Somehow before our match with the Lehigh Rugby Club, we're warming up and the conversation turns to individuals that possess an ability to urinate great distances.

Our back-up quarterback, Rick "The Fire Hose" Mason is the stuff legends are made of. Rick can piss like a race horse with tremendous velocity and distance. We are bragging him up when a Lehigh player with the number six on his brown and white jersey states emphatically, "We have a guy that can out-piss your Fire Hose any day of the week."

Not one to back away from a challenge I propose a bet, "Oh yeah? How about a wager?"

"Alright, the loser buys pizza for both teams," declares #6.

"You and your lightweight tinkler have a bet," I shot back.

Fire Hose is going to look more like a garden hose when King Schlong cuts loose," says #6.

Nice play on words...King Kong...King Schlong.

"Dream on Lehigh. Enough of your jive. We'll let our piss do the talkin." I reply.

 For Rick, the rugby match became inconsequential. We keep him on the sidelines to drink and eat throughout the match. It's important for him to build up as much pressure internally as he can. Therefore in nonstop fashion he continues to guzzle down anything we have with us, especially beer. I'm amazed at the amount of beer, water, pretzels and potato chips that Rick devours. He is a non-stop eating and drinking machine.

At the conclusion of the match both sides can't wait to get to the main event that's billed as the Great Pizza Piss-off. Around seventy-five players and spectators from both teams wait to see the outcome of the "whiz war". The buzz from the remaining crowd is electrifying. The Lehigh guy, King Schlong steps up onto the two-foot high bench, drops his pants and lets out a five-foot long stream while his Lehigh contingent cheers him wildly.

Not to be outdone the Allentown Club goes berserk as Rick the Fire Hose ascends the platform. The Allentown crowd yells out numerous words of encouragement to motivate Rick.

"Roll out the fire hose, Rick!"

"The Prince of Piss will double your dribble!"

"Drain the dragon all over Lehigh!"

"Rick, you are the freak of leak...the Urinator!"

In a trance, Rick methodically steps up on the platform with a look of total concentration on his face. Slowly he lowers his shorts until they drop to his ankles. After three seconds of clutching and squeezing his penis to build up the last measure of pressure, Rick suddenly releases the flow. What could only be described as a multi-oriface explosion, all of Rick's bodily functions erupt at the same time. Simultaneously a nine-foot stream of urine gushes from his dick like a geyser, while diarrhea spews from his ass down his legs and onto his shorts.

We're ecstatic that the Fire Hose destroys King Schlong. Clearly Rick displayed the badder bladder. However we're approximately thirty yards from the nearest building. That's one of the loneliest walks I've witnessed as Rick shuffles his feet the entire distance with his shit-covered shorts around his ankles. After he cleans himself up we all have a good laugh. He defended his crown and won us all free pizza.

> So what if he shit himself. Rick never lost sight of the goal. More of us need to display that kind of commitment and accountability if the Mules are going to succeed.

While football is my first love I come to appreciate the sport of rugby. My experience with the sport inspires me to write a poem entitled **Rugby**.

> "On the hill the spectators viewed, but they did not see.
>
> Cheering the brutality: they didn't have to feel
>
> the pain of the fallen warrior.
>
> I was moved to sickness as blood sprang to
>
> decorate the green and brown arena.
>
> Of no importance to me was the fact his shirt differed in color from mine.

Each proud gladiator that acted on that grassy stage was bonded by the parallel desires to compete, survive and ponder why.

Some play to achieve a playground immortality, some to fantasize manhood, yet others to escape the external.

Muscle against muscle, hit countered by hit, grunt for grunt, spinning, slashing, smashing.

It's a total expression: your body speaks, it laughs, it cries and if you are lucky enough to win, it's a release of unequalled emotion.

As you dance across the goal line, a natural zenith is sustained.

Suddenly the leather treasure is the most exquisite, harmonious, pleasing, phenomenon in the universe.

Hugged to the point of explosion, it is finally pilfered by a black-striped policeman.

Outsiders yell, scream, slap backs and shake hands.

But by Wednesday all is erased from their memories, lost sight of and forgotten.

As all foolish, futile games should be.

Why then do some men choose to portray Spartans and risk injury over the senseless?

Because of a need.

A need to shed school, responsibilities and reality.

On Saturdays I sprint, cut, rock, explode, absorb, tackle, catch, pass and fly; I am an artist in a ballet of spikes.

After much beer, song and pool with exhausted comrades it's time to come down to the normal, the sensible, the burdensome.

But for two hours it's a wonderful love affair between thirty men and a pregnant football."

I'm honored to discover my poem is selected for entry into the spring **Arcade** magazine, Muhlenberg College's formal publication recognizing artistic endeavors. It consists of poems, short stories and photographs that a panel of faculty members select. Some bias against jocks exists on campus so my selection comes as a complete surprise, albeit a welcome one.

Two weeks later, as I complete my last exam in Russian Literature, my thoughts turn to the Jersey Shore. This summer adventure will prove to be the foundation upon which we build our future success.

Chapter Thirteen   "Sore at the Shore"

We turn off the Jersey Parkway at Exit 63 and head east on Route 72 with the top down on my '60 Caddy. Seals and Croft's Summer Breeze is playing on the radio.

> "Summer breeze, makes me feel fine, blowing through the jasmine in my mind.
> Summer breeze, makes me feel fine, blowing through the jasmine in my mind.
>
> Sweet days of summer, the jasmine's in bloom.
> July is dressed up and playing her tune.
> And I come home from a hard day's work, and you're waiting there, not a care in the world."

"How great is this? The school year is done and we're gonna be at the Jersey Shore all summer. This is cool city," says Robbie Boll.

"You're right-on, Boll-man. Your Uncle was awesome to let us stay at his boarding house and give us a break on the rent. He's one good dude," I reply as our caravan of automobiles crosses over the half-mile long causeway onto Long Beach Island. As we travel over the bay it's a total kick-ass party for the senses; the distinctive smell of salt water, the welcoming cries of seagulls, the ocean breeze passing gently across our faces and the stunning blue horizon.

We reach 12th street in Surf City and start moving our stuff into our summer digs. The former boarding house is a four-story Victorian structure with a large wrap-around porch, multiple steep roof pitches, and a turret right down the middle of the building. While it's in need of some repair, we love the house and with fifteen bedrooms and six bathrooms it's perfect to accommodate our 'Berg gang. Paul Palmisano and I race to grab one of the bedrooms in the turret. Tank, Paul's twin Arnie and "the Jet" claim the big room right across from ours.

Living in a tower is one bad pad!

If we're going to make this shore gig work for our conditioning efforts we need to coordinate our schedules. That's the main topic at our first house meeting on the massive front porch. Everyone put their work schedules on the picnic table and we analyzed what would be best to support our team workouts.

After careful review I conclude, "Ah it looks like the primo times for our workouts are at 7:00 in the morning and at 5:30 in the afternoon. "

"If any one of us miss a team workout we must do an individual session as a make-up," says Tank.

"We passed a gym right as we got off the causeway in Ship Bottom on 8th Street. Let's lay a rap down and see if they'll give us a deal for the summer," The Jet adds.

In full agreement I say, "Ok, Jet and I will run down and shoot the breeze with the owners."

The name of the gym is Lyceum, a no-frills establishment but as we tour it we find it has everything we need; free weights, power racks, dumbbells, cables, Nautilus, etc. The owner is very accommodating and gives us a summer rate of $10 per month per person.

With the gym memberships in hand, we come up with the following regimen to prepare ourselves for the upcoming season.

> Monday, Wednesday and Friday mornings – weightlifting at Lyceum (shoulders, lats, and arms)
>
> Tuesday and Thursday mornings – weightlifting at Lyceum (legs and chest)
>
> Monday, Wednesday, Friday and Saturday afternoons – running and cardiovascular conditioning
>
> Tuesday and Thursday afternoons – For those sessions we agree to use our creativity and each of us will take a turn to design a set of physical trials to challenge our stamina and mental toughness.
>
> Sunday would be for rest, recuperation and relaxation.
>
> *Let's face it. We're at the Jersey shore. Gotta have some fun.*

The next day, I start my job at the Sandbar Miniature Golf Course. Luckily it's only a couple of blocks over from our house. The job seems like a real gas. I get to work with kids and part of my job is to always have music blaring over our loudspeaker to ensure an upbeat, fun atmosphere. Tuesdays turn out to be my favorite day because we run a weekly golf tournament, The Ocean Open with the tagline, "Be a Superstar at the Sandbar." We have an entry fee of $1 and pay out cash awards for the lowest five scorers in addition to raffle prizes like season passes for free golf. If the weather is good, we attract thirty to forty kids.

I get a real kick out of making a production of the award ceremonies. We devised a multi-tiered podium where we present medals and take instant Polaroid photos of the winners. We give one snapshot to the kids and we post one in our clubhouse where we maintain a summer collage of winners.

After the first week, we all get into a good groove with our jobs and workout schedules. Since I had visited LBI numerous times in the past, I'm given the responsibility of coming up with the first creative workout.

"Guys, get ready to go down to Barnegat Light House. We're going to do the stairs there," I proclaim.

"Cobber, are you sure that's a good idea? It's ninety-degrees out and it will be probably near one hundred degrees in the tube," Arnie says.

"Listen pussy-willow, we came to the shore to challenge ourselves. So paste on your tiny little mouse balls and let's go!" I shout back.

"Yeah Arnie, don't disgrace the Palmisano name. Get your Converse on and let's move," his twin brother Paul chimes in.

It's about a fifteen minute ride from Surf City to Old Barney, the nickname for the brick lighthouse located on the northern most point of LBI. It rises 165 feet above the ground with the bottom half of the tower painted white and the top half painted red. Lt. General George Mead was placed in charge of designing the lighthouse and completed the project in 1859. Mead was famous for leading the Union troops at the Battle of Gettysburg.

Old Barney's purpose was to enable safe passage through the Barnegat Inlet for trade and travel. After World War II it was decommissioned and eventually turned over to the State of New Jersey and the surrounding area has been converted into a state park. It is the second tallest lighthouse in the United States.

There are 217 steps from the bottom of the Lighthouse to the top where there is a small, circular observation deck. The interior is extremely tight. Only two people can fit the narrow width so essentially it is single file up and single file down. We purposely go earlier in the day to avoid tourist traffic and therefore essentially have the Lighthouse to ourselves.

"OK Mules, we're going to climb this tower fifteen times. Let Jet and Boll get upfront to lead us and you bigger dudes in the rear," Captain Jon orders.

Knowing we've got to climb this baby single file, Jon wants the smaller, faster guys in the lead. Today is a sweltering 92-degrees and we're really feeling the heat. While the first climb's pace was between a walk and a slight jog, our thighs quickly turn to cement and the workout transforms into a survival exercise. The lighthouse narrows at the top and with twenty players giving off our own personal heat the lighthouse becomes unbearably hot. There are two spots in the tower that a person can get off to the side and rest on a platform if one is too tired to continue.

After five climbs we have to create ways to motivate ourselves to keep going. After I had completed eight climbs the Tasmanian Devil and I took turns slapping each other's face and shouting insults as if we are POWs.

"You vill climb those steps you piece of human fecal matter," we shout in our best Sergeant Shultz German accent from the TV show Hogan's Heroes.

 Some of the guys start singing the song, **Go All the Way** by the Raspberries to spur them to keep moving.

> "I never knew how complete love could be
> Till she kissed me and said
> Baby, please, **go all the way**
> It feels so right
> Being with you here tonight
> Please, **go all the way**"

It gets a bit dicey when Tank and Chuck Biers start "cutting the cheese" at the halfway mark. They had salami and brats with sauerkraut for lunch. You can imagine what their farts smelled like, sort of puke sandwiched between two full baby diapers sitting atop raw sewage.

"Tank, what the fuck did you do? Shit your pants?!?" shouts Arnie.

"It's not my fault. This climbing bullshit shook up my insides. Blame Corn-Cobb, that flaming asshole," Tank replies as he moves off to the side on the mid-way platform. Each of us takes turns punching him in the arm as we pass Tank on the way up as a small piece of revenge for making the lighthouse smell like a Nebraska pig farm. Chuck keeps moving so he misses our retaliation.

What was he saying about a flaming asshole? Smells like he's got one burning right now...

Our first climb was probably completed in five minutes or less. Ultimately because of the tight quarters and extreme temperature it takes us over two hours to complete the fifteen climbs with the occasional water break. We're all very proud of Tank because this ordeal is much more challenging for a two-hundred and sixty-five pounder than for most of us. We all give encouragement to Tank as he works through his last two agonizing repetitions. A huge cheer goes up as Tank makes his descent on the fifteenth interval.

It feels like rigor mortis has attacked our thighs. But the sense of accomplishment feels tremendous and it's moments like these that will inspire us to achieve great things in the future.

Go Mules!

To treat ourselves for what we had just achieved at Old Barney, we stop at the Shellfish Company in Harvey Cedars. The Restaurant is styled after a 1920's beach house and it's known for mouthwatering, fresh seafood. We grab takeout and cook it up later that evening.

After two weeks of grueling workouts, we decide to have some fun on Saturday night. While not everyone in the house is 21, between possessing fake IDs and making friends with most of the bartenders on the strip we get into all the joints we want to.

The boys are psyched for a pub crawl so we arrange to have a party bus take us up and down the island. The party bus has been advertised in the Beachcomber magazine as Babe's Booze Bus. According to LBI gossip, this guy, a Minnesota transplant, bought an old school bus and painted it blue in honor of Paul Bunyan's Babe the Blue Ox. He rents the bus and himself out to groups that want to party but not drive.

We have the bus all night, and to keep the party moving in-between stops a keg of Miller Light is strategically placed in the back seat. We start at the Acme Hotel where they have 10-cent beers. We move to Kubels in Barnegat Light and on to the Gateway Bar. Near 11:30 PM we arrive at 20th Street in Ship Bottom, the home of Joe Pop's Bar. A nightclub that's always had a lot of action and this night is no exception. All three bar sections are overflowing with foxy mamas. A local band called The Personifiers are playing Edgar Winter Group's Free Ride as we saunter in.

> "The mountain is high, the valley is low
> And you're confused 'bout which way to go
> So I flew here to give you a hand
> And lead you into the Promised Land
>
> So, come on and take a free ride (free ride)
> Come on and take it by my side
> Come on and take a free ride"

"This place is happening!" says Jet.

"Man I'm tripping with all these chicks," adds Arnie.

"Well let's dive in boys. Don't be lightweights and sit with your thumbs up your asses. Let's boogie with some young ladies."

Paul is first to ask a chick to dance but is shot down. "What a drag Paulie. She must have sensed your freakishly small dick," his twin says.

"Hey, don't worry about me spaz-boy. They don't call me the Italian Stallion for nothing. Plus I'm the best looking guy in the joint," Paul replies.

"Okay girls, don't get your panties in a bunch. Just keep swinging the bats," Chuck says.

Tank, totally buzzed throws his arms around me and after belching in my face exclaims, "Wazzup suckas! Yous guys gonna boogie or what?"

Arnie makes a hit with a cute chick, Peggy from Bayonne. She is staying with girlfriends for the summer and works as a carhop at the A & W Drive-in near Brant Beach. Arnie is really the only one that gets serious action that night. The rest of us whoop it up with multiple chicks but not much magic is happening.

Paul and I ask the Babe Booze Bus driver to take us back to our pad around 1:30 AM. I've got the afternoon shift at the Sandbar tomorrow which means it is my responsibility to close the course. Feeling tired and wasted, I start to board the bus just as I see Scott, the Prize Hog, trying to walk Tank to the bus. Ten yards from the bus Tank bends over and spews his guts out. It looks like a volcano erupting as his projectile vomiting just misses Scott's leg.

We have two final riders as Arnie and Peggy decide to come with us.

> *I would be lying if I didn't admit I was a little jealous of A-Palmisano.*

This long-legged, brunette with more curves than a Dorney Park roller coaster is hanging all over Arnie. She is an Adrienne Barbeau look-alike, the gorgeous TV daughter on the hit TV series, Maude.

To make us even more envious Arnie has the biggest shit-eating grin on his face as he and Peggy sit together on the ride home. His smirk resembles that of Burt Reynolds when he posed nude for Cosmopolitan Magazine last year with his forearm strategically placed to hide his privates. Arnie won't need a forearm to maintain modesty. His pinky will probably suffice.

> *Jealousy really does make you say ugly things.*

We all flop into our rooms while Arnie entertains Leggy-Peggy in our living room. They appear to be half watching a movie and half making out. Paul and I can't leave things alone. It's part of our inalienable rights of life, liberty and the pursuit of busting Arnie's balls. So we mastermind the following plan. We would walk through the living room and totally ignore the couple, but with each pass of the room we would take off articles of clothing. At this point between all the beer we've consumed and the prospects of embarrassing Arnie, we are absolutely stoked.

The first time around we take off our shirts and prance through the room. Arnie attempts to hide Peggy's eyes so as not to let her see what real men look like. At first Arnie laughs with us, but as it sinks in that we're going to continue to progressively strip down he becomes extremely nervous.

Just before the fourth pass we're down to jocks. I explore Biers' room because he works as a security guard and owns some paraphernalia that could be fun. I pin his badge to my jock and don his cop hat and dark glasses. Then I take out his nightstick and pepper spray, and proceed to march into the living room with Paul in tow sporting our athletic supporters. Arnie sees us before Peggy and goes into full panic mode.

Acting like a cop I exclaim in my best Smokey voice, "You in a whole lotta trouble, Boy." At that point Arnie calls us butt wipes for ruining his evening and literally tosses Peggy down the stairs to the first floor and is quickly escorting her to his car.

Paul and I can't leave it at that. We have one last raunchy act of vulgarity to insure Arnie will never forget this night. The window of my room on the second story overlooks our parking lot. Paul comes up with the idea to moon the squeamish couple. Without hesitation I plant my ample derriere on the windowsill just as Arnie opens up the car door. Paul is directly across from me bench-pressing my shoulders to make my butt cheeks smoosh even more. Paul is looking out the window and giving me a blow-by-blow description of what was happening because all I can see is Paul's face literally inches from mine and we're laughing hysterically. He informs me that Arnie is looking up. I have never laughed as hard in my life as I did in that moment

I shout in-between gasps of laughter, "Paul, stop pushing I have to go the bathroom!"

Paul completely disregards my pleas and continues to push as hard as he possibly can.

"I'm not kidding. I'm gonna shit right here!" I squeal still convulsing and snorting with laughter.

"Sure Cobber, I am too," replies Paul disregarding my vigorous pleas.

"I really mean it! I just SHIT ON THE WINDOW!" I scream.

"Yeah, I just shit too!" Paul says in a mocking tone.

Finally I push him aside and sure enough situated on the sill is a little surprise poop. We continue to laugh for what seems to be hours. The muscles along my ribcage hurt for days.

Those authors of Greek comedies like Aristophanes knew what they were doing when they used vulgarity and human frailties to make a comedic impact. Poop stories always make people laugh.

Wow…. my World Literature class is really paying off.

For almost a year, the country has been caught up in the Watergate proceedings but on Saturday, June 9th 1973, as we lay around our living room, the collective mindset of the entire nation forgets about the Washington scandal and is totally focused on a majestic horse named Secretariat attempting to win the coveted Triple Crown. This muscular, copper chestnut thoroughbred enters Belmont Park having won both the Kentucky Derby and the Preakness Stakes. No horse has won the Triple Crown in 25 years since Citation in 1948.

What strikes me as we watch Secretariat enter the starting gate is he has the look of a champion. Standing sixty-six inches high and weighing 1200 pounds, this magnificent animal exudes confidence. The Announcer, George Cassidy shouts, "They're off!" and the five horses bunch together around the first turn. By the second turn it is a two-horse race with Secretariat holding a length and a-half lead over Sham. By the back stretch, Secretariat begins to pour it on and drives to a world record of 2 minutes and 24 seconds over the mile and a-half course. This special champion wins by a record 31 lengths and his jockey, Ron Turcotte, claims that he lost control of his horse and that Secretariat dashed into destiny on his own.

Standing in the Winner's Circle, covered in a blanket of white carnations, the three-year old colt appears to know that he's made history. Secretariat looks fearless snorting from his white triangle-marked head and white-striped nose.

We've witnessed greatness and if the Mules are going to win we need to find that same intensity and focus.

Motivated by Secretariat's performance, we go down to the 14th Street sand dunes and begin to challenge ourselves on the beach. Captain Jon Lambert leads us as we perform repetitions of sprinting up and walking down the sandy summit. In short order we're sweating profusely. Wearing only shorts and sneakers we complete thirty sprints in about 45 minutes. Once we finish the hill work, we continue the workout with up-downs in the sand. While jogging in place on Jon's command, we kick back our legs and throw our chests onto the beach and immediately bounce back up. Because we're covered in perspiration it takes only one up-down to completely cover our bodies in sand. The other shore patrons lying on their blankets really enjoy the spectacle. We look like a crazy tribe of Sahara Desert nomads, but the sense of accomplishment feels good.

To give the beach spectators a little thrill, we end up performing a Pacific Islander war chant called the Haka. Since being introduced to the sport of rugby I've become fascinated with the best rugby team in the world, the All Blacks of New Zealand. Competing on the international scene since 1903, the New Zealanders have maintained the tradition of performing the Haka before competitions as an attempt to intimidate their opposition. It is a war chant that originated with the Māori people of eastern Polynesia.

We form three lines with me out in front. I squat into a three-quarter stance with my arms flexed one over the other in front of my sand-crusted chest and my teammates follow suit in unison. I yell out a preparatory instruction, "Ringa pakia!" and we begin slapping our knees, then our forearms, then pointing towards the sky we chant alternately at the top of our lungs.

"Ka mate! Ka mate! (I die, I die)

Ka ora! Ka ora! (I live, I live)

Ka mate! Ka mate!" (I die, I die)"

Ka ora! Ka ora! (I live, I live) "

All together ending with foot stomps we scream "Whiti te rā (The sun shines) and Hī! (Rise). The last move is to stick out our tongues to create an intimidating effect.

While we're fully cognizant of the fact that we're bastardizing a proper Haka, in our own way we're honoring the Māori culture with a Jersey twist. We've got nothing but respect for the true warriors.

Our Haka prompts a spontaneous round of applause from the onlooking sun worshipers. We use that encouragement to sprint towards the ocean waves and dive head-first in the foamy, white-capped surf.

Ah, that feels unbelievable.

Chapter Fourteen

"We meet The Boss"

Chet the Jet is the guy in the house who always keeps us connected to what's happening on the music scene. He starts telling us about a musician he's seen at the Upstage Club in Asbury Park named Bruce Springsteen. Earlier this year Bruce and his E-street Band released their first album **Greetings from Asbury Park, NJ.** The Jet is constantly playing Springsteen's songs from the album.

One day in early June, Jet sprints into the house and yells, "Hey guys, get down here!"

"What's up?" Chuck asks.

"Fat City in Seaside Heights is hosting Bruce Springsteen on June 23rd. Tickets are only $4.50. We can't miss this scene. The band's sound is way cool," Chet explains passionately.

We take roll call to see who wants to go and who could go taking into account work schedules. Twelve of us give Chet the greenlight to buy the tickets. We're all gassed to see this rocker in person that Chet has talked up so much.

"Go get'em Jet. It's gonna be da bomb...funkadelic!" Tank exclaimed.

When the day of the show arrives, the twelve of us stuff ourselves in two cars and head north on the Garden State Parkway. Fat City is located between Hamilton

Avenue and the Boulevard. It's bitchin' to the max where fans can get up close and personal with the performers. We're a little late and Springsteen is already on stage. Standing before us is a skinny dude sporting a thin mustache, a tuft of hair under his lower lip leading to a short beard around his chin with curly black hair. His voice is gravelly and soulful. As we enter the show, Bruce is in the middle of a new song he's trying out on the crowd entitled Rosalita. He rocks out the refrain,

> "Rosalita jump a little lighter
> Senorita come sit by my fire
> I just want to be your love, ain't no lie
> Rosalita you're my stone desire."

It's an amazing show that lasts over three hours. Bruce's endurance is feakish. After a couple encores the final song, Blinded by the Light is so far out it blows our minds.

> "Madman drummers bummers and Indians in the summer with a teenage diplomat
> In the dumps with the mumps as the adolescent pumps his way into his hat
> With a boulder on my shoulder, feelin' kinda older I tripped the merry-go-round
> With this very unpleasing sneezing and wheezing the calliope crashed to the ground
> Some all-hot half-shot was headin' for a hot spot snappin' his fingers clappin' his hands
> And some fleshpot mascot was tied into a lover's knot with a whatnot in her hand
> And now young Scott with a slingshot finally found a tender spot and throws his lover in the sand

And some bloodshot forget-me-not whispers,
"Daddy's within earshot, save the buckshot, turn
up the band

And she was blinded by the light
Oh, cut loose like a deuce another runner in the
night
Blinded by the light
She got down but she never got tight, but she'll
make it alright..."

I wondered how Springsteen got the nickname, The Boss. I learned later that it was his job to collect the money from the early gigs in the sixties and distribute the money among the band members. As a result they began calling him The Boss and the name stuck. That story may be true but in my mind it's the way Bruce commanded the stage tonight is what truly makes him The Boss.

Chet the Jet talks his way backstage past the bouncers by saying he and I handle the equipment. There are about twenty-five people crowded in what looks to be a dressing room. The Boss is holding court with some groupies when The Jet works his way near Bruce.

"Bruce, I know every record and song you've done. I've got a cousin who lives in Freehold Borough where you grew up. He took me to see you play with the Castiles at Café Wha? in Manhattan. I love your stuff," Chet the Jet proudly proclaims.

"Glad you hip to the groove cuz, "Bruce says. And then he offers us a couple of beers. Chet went on to pay homage to The Boss by naming every song on the

Greetings from Asbury Park album. Bruce is amused by Chet's fanaticism and shares a piece of advice with us, "Boyz whatever you choose to do in this life...do it with passion. And don't let others' bullshit stop you from doing what you believe in. Stay true to your journey."

Truer words for the Mules have never been spoken. We needed to realize our vision of being a winning football team and not let any distractions or naysayers block our path. We stay about 20 minutes and then rush out to catch up with the guys and tell them about our run in with The Boss.

Chapter Fifteen

"Watergate / Water Date"

We've got about a month and a half until we head back to College for preseason two-a-day workouts. Living at the shore has brought us closer together as a team and provided the right environment to get us in the best shape of our lives. However, not all the creative conditioning sessions worked out as planned. We had major concerns when Fire Hose suggested we should row kayaks.

This afternoon we head north on the island to Bobbie's Boat rentals on 7th Street in Barnegat Light. We rent five tandem kayaks for two hours and devise a tag-team competition. Each squad is comprised of four guys. The first set of competitors start in the kayaks and race against the other four kayaks to a designated buoy. Then they race back to the dock line and hand-off the kayak to their two remaining team members.

It was my misfortune to be paired with Tank. We never had a chance.

"Have you ever rowed a kayak before Big Man?" I ask.

"Nah, but how freaking hard could it be," Tank replies.

I began to say, "Balance is import..." but Tank interrupts and smugly says, "Don't be a little bitch, you doubting dickhead."

"Alright fuckface...but let Boll and Biers go first. We'll take the second lap," I reply.

Arnie shouted, "On your mark...get set...go!" The five kayaks race out of the starting gate. Other than Boll most of us hadn't done much kayaking before and it shows. Kayaks are tipping and bobbing all over the place. It doesn't help that we allow fighting between the crews.

Boll and Biers make it back to the dock first. Tank and I are poised for the exchange. I get in the kayak first. Then Tank steps in and immediately his legs begin wobbling as he fights unsuccessfully to maintain his balance. The kayak flips over and Tank erupts with a stream of obscenities. Our performance doesn't get better the entire afternoon. I find out later that the kayaks have a maximum weight recommendation of three-hundred and ninety pounds and collectively we weigh around four-hundred and fifty pounds. Needless to say that's the first and last time we're going to use kayaks as part of our conditioning efforts.

Driving back from Bobbies Boat Rentals, I can't help but notice how the subject of Watergate is on everybody's minds. Ever since last June when five men were arrested for breaking-into the Democratic National Committee headquarters at the Watergate office complex in Washington, DC it has dominated the news.

On the radio, the newscaster announces that President Nixon refused today to turn over presidential tape recordings that might shed information into his role in the scandal. At the same time we pass Sari Harari, a clothing shop in Viking Village and they are advertising a Watergate sale with sinking prices. Indian print dresses for two dollars. With everybody getting into the Watergate act Wolfman comes up with the idea of WaterDate.

Gigi and Debbie along with a few other girlfriends are coming to LBI for a visit. His idea is to break into the Colony Movie Theater on 35th Street in Brant Beach.

When we pitch the WaterDate idea to the girls it's met initially with resistance.

"You want us to sneak into the movies without paying? That's nothing to do with a Watergate theme, that's just because you are the cheapest buttheads in the world," Gigi replies.

"Well if you don't like that idea I have another, Water Mate. Under the cloak of darkness we sneak into the ocean and make love until someone catches us," Wolfman jokes.

"If that's the alternative give me the movies," Gigi shoots back sarcastically.

The movie at the Colony is Live and Let Die. The eighth James Bond thriller but the first with Roger Moore as the lead actor.

Nobody did it better than Sean Connery.

Three couples decide to experience Water Date; Gigi and Gregg, Kevin Cornwell (Corny) and his girlfriend Sally and Debbie and I. We all dress in black clothing to make us more stealth and to accentuate the covert nature of this plan. Arnie Palmisano is to be our Gordon Liddy, the architect of the operation. We give him money to buy a ticket and it's his job to stake out the side exit door and let us know when it's safe to infiltrate the complex.

The six of us hide as best we can behind a dumpster. The girls can't help themselves from giggling throughout our concealment. After what seems to be an eternity but is actually closer to fifteen minutes, the exit door cracks open and Arnie whispers with a sense of urgency, "Get in here now."

Without incident we quickly transition to our seats and enjoy the Bond flick although the best part of the evening is the feeling of pulling off the WaterDate caper.

After the show we stop for crab cake sandwiches and beers at the Surf City Hotel. Debbie maintains that the whole WaterDate idea is a scam and that we're just too cheap to buy tickets. She probably isn't far off because we finish the evening at the Sandbar with Miniature Golf where I have free passes. What's wrong with frugality? I believe it was Confucius that said, "He who does not economize will have to agonize."

Chapter Sixteen

"New uses for tires"

It's the first Monday in August and we are experiencing mixed emotions as we sit around the living room. On one hand, we are sad to see the summer coming to an end, but on the other hand we are anxious to start football camp in a week and a half. Collectively we are in the best shape of our lives and it's time to put the fruits of our labor to work on the gridiron.

The morning edition of the New Jersey Star Ledger reminds me that today Roberto Clemente, one of my childhood heroes is being inducted posthumously into the Baseball Hall of Fame making him the first Latin American ever to be afforded that honor. Roberto represents one of only two Hall of Fame members for whom the mandatory five-year waiting period has been waived, the other being Lou Gehrig.

While Roberto Clemente was a great hitter, it was his fielding and arm that left a lasting impression on me. He earned twelve consecutive Gold Glove Awards for his excellence in right field and rarely did base runners try to take an extra base on his arm. Tim McCarver, catcher for the St. Louis Cardinals, said it best, "Some right fielders have rifles for arms, but he had a howitzer."

Fittingly, Roberto will enter the Hall of Fame with Monte Irvin, a great black player who enjoyed early success in the Negro Leagues with the Newark Eagles and was only the fifth black player ever to compete in the major leagues. It's great to see the Hall paying the proper respect to deserving individuals regardless of their skin color or place of origin. We have come a long way as a country, but we have a long way to go to resolve the injustices that still exist with gender and race.

As a group of us eat breakfast I share my sentiment, "It's great to see Roberto Clemente going into the Hall of Fame. No one deserves it more. He was the whole package."

"Yea, it's hard to believe he is no longer with us," replies Paul.

"He was a real hero that made the ultimate sacrifice. How many people would fly out on New Year's Eve with relief supplies for earthquake victims with just himself and a pilot?" Arnie adds.

"And that was no one time deal. Clemente had a long history of doing charity work for his home country of Puerto Rico. He never forgot his humble beginnings. I believe his father worked in the sugar fields for a living." Paul shared.

"As a kid Roberto worked in those same fields with his pop to help put food on the table. He had five brothers and a sister." Chuck said.

"It's that kind of dedication and perseverance that separates greatness from mediocrity." I said.

At that moment Ron Wood and Frankie Johnson, our black teammates come into the room. Ron and Frankie hailed from Brooklyn, New York. They both attended Brooklyn Tech High School but Frankie was a year younger. Ron (#42) was a six-foot-three, two-hundred and twenty-five pound fullback who was bigger than most of us linemen. Usually wearing his hair in cornrows his nickname was Long Wood. Some say he was pegged with the name for his substantial height while others maintain that it was attributed to his impressive male appendage. Either way the moniker worked. Frankie (#64) was one of the quickest defensive ends in the league. Barely six- foot and two hundred pounds, Frankie made up for his modest size with incredible quickness and a nose for the ball. He was always around the action.

"Our last creative workout is coming up. Gotta do something memorable," Ron said.

"Let's have you, me and Chuck get together and bust our ass on it," I said. My reason for wanting Chuck involved was because he has a job with Tuckerton Lumber Company on the island. He can get us anything from the hardware store if we need it.

The three of us go into my bedroom and I share an idea I have regarding an abandoned construction site near Maris Stella Retreat in Harvey Cedars. The Retreat has been run by the Sisters of Charity Saint Elizabeth since 1959 providing spiritual nourishment to its visitors. The Retreat, one of the most beautiful locations on LBI, consists of a collection of pristine white buildings including a chapel and conference center upon ten beautifully landscaped acres.

Adjacent to Maris Stella is a construction site that for the time being is no longer active. What caught my eye was a number of tires just laying around on the premises. And a couple of those tires are so huge they must have come off a large skid loader. I estimate them to be about five feet high and two feet wide.

"Hey guys. What if we set up a circuit of creative exercises with the tires on that abandoned lot near the Sister's Retreat?" I said.

"It's got potential Cobber," Chuck offers back.

"Cool...let's go there sometime tomorrow to scout out what we can do," adds Ron.

The next day, the three of us tour the site and after much deliberation and exploration designed what we think would be a gauntlet of physical torture that will challenge us to the max.

When the last Thursday rolls around, the guys are amazed with what we had devised. Our circuit encompasses six independent stations. First off is the tire flip which is just what it sounds like. You squat down and get a good grip on what we estimated to be a four hundred pound tire and you lift and flip it over. You try to get as many flips in a minute as you can. Every station was timed to be a minute long. Second, you have to do pull-ups on a low-hanging branch of a tree that is situated on the site. We placed a box under the tree because when guys get too tired to pull themselves up they can jump up and lower themselves slowly working the muscles in a negative fashion as they resist on the way down. Third is a series of twenty car tires that each person had to run through alternating one foot at a time, doing that as many times back and forth for a minute. Station four is called sledge hits. You take a sixteen pound sledge hammer that Chuck borrowed from Tuckerton Lumber and you hit a large earthmover tire propped up against a tree with a lateral swing. Again you do that as many times as you can for a minute. The last two stations are designed to kill the legs. Fifth station is a tire drag exercise nicknamed the Mule Train whereby you pull backwards approximately a two hundred pound tire with a chain and drag it as far as you can for a minute. If ever there was an appropriate exercise for a Mule it is this one. We are truly honoring the beast of burden. Again Chuck helped us out with work gloves from his Tuckerton store. Lastly is the dreaded tire jump. With exhausted legs at this point you have to jump in and out of a large earthmover tire for a minute.

Two people are at each station. One guy performs the exercise while the other rests. Once each pair has completed that particular station, they move on to the next exercise. There are twenty-two of us in attendance that day. Ron knows Sister Mary at Maris Stella and she gave him permission for us to use an isolated part of their property that is adjacent to the abandoned construction site for our special workout day if we need extra space.

With the temperature hovering in the 80's accompanied by 45% humidity, the conditions provide a challenging environment for us to do our tire circuit training. Our goal is to get everyone through the entire circuit six times. That would represent 30 minutes of concentrated, strenuous activity.

We start at 4:00 PM in the afternoon and it takes us until just before 6:30 PM to get everyone through the complete circuit five times. I could not imagine sweating any more than we did that day. All of us are completely drenched. We brought water with us and drank generously throughout the session but most of us still lost between 5 and 8 pounds of water weight that afternoon. Tank actually lost 12 pounds of water.

"Great work guys. We are gonna kick some ass in the MAC!" yells Captain Jon Lambert referring to our Mid Atlantic Conference foes.

"Gimme five!" shouts the Tasmanian Devil as he runs around high-fiving everybody. The wrestlers never let themselves get out of shape. Wolfman and Devil feasted on the circuit training.

Everyone is exhausted but the feeling of pride is palpable. With one last burst of energy Paul yells out, "Last one in the ocean is a pussy!" And with that, he races across the boulevard from the bayside to the ocean side and heads towards the sea. We all follow suit because we couldn't wait to feel the ocean waves cool our bodies down.

"Man, water has never felt so good on my body. Can you dig it?" Frankie exclaims.

"I can dig it all day, Frankie," said Chuck.

We played in the waves until a somewhat irate homeowner informs us that this is a private beach. Everyone remains cool with the situation because we had gotten what we came for. However, Tank inadvertently moons the guy as he walks towards the street.

"It was a harmless mistake, my shorts' drawstring loosened with all the exercise," Tank snickered.

It seemed reasonable to me that his drawstring might give way against the forces of gravity and his massive abdominal girth.

As we return to the house, The Odd Couple with Tony Randall (Felix Unger) and Jack Klugman (Oscar Madison) is playing on the boob tube. In this episode, Felix wants to be on the TV Password Game Show with Alan Ludden at all costs and when he finally gets on the show through Oscar's connections, Felix makes a huge fool of himself. I split a gut when Felix refuses to leave the stage even after he loses the game.

I finish watching the Odd Couple and get ready for our last evening of the summer vacation before we travel back home over the weekend and get ready for football camp next week.

As I shower, competing songs blast from two rooms. Long Wood is listening to **Keep on Truckin** by Eddie Kendricks while Prize Hog is playing Grand Funk Railroad's **We're an American Band**.

"Out on the road for forty days Last night in Little Rock, put me in a haze Sweet, sweet Connie was doin' her act She had the whole	"Baby, it's bad It's so hard to bear Yes, babe You're hard to bear I've got a fever rising with desire It's my love jones and I feel like I'm

show and that's a
natural fact

Up all night with
Freddie King
I got to tell you,
poker's his thing
Booze and ladies,
keep me right
As long as we can
make it to the show
tonight

We're an American
band
We're an American
band
We're comin' to
your town
We'll help you party
it down
We're an American
band"

on fire

And I'll keep on
keep on truckin,
baby
I got to keep on
truckin
Got to get to your
good lovin
Huh... huh... huh...
huh... huh...

Feelin good
No, you can't stop
the feelin
No, you can't stop
the feelin
No, not now

Paul met someone through the gym that has a private
beach near North Lane in Loveladies and his friend
invites us over for beers. To our shock when we arrive at
the designated address...the house is actually a friggin'
mansion. Apparently this dude, Gregg Buxton, has very
wealthy parents. It's our good fortune that this week
Gregg has the house all to himself.

There is a state-of-the-art stereo system playing on the
patio and a fire has been started on the beach. Even
though we bring beer with us, Gregg has a keg tapped

near the fire. We have died and gone to heaven. Feeling the aftereffects of the tire circuit, we are happy to just bullshit around the fire and drink beer all night. All the stories of the summer get bigger and better with each beer we down. Originally we had planned to head to Joe Pops Bar after midnight, but none of us rally. Gregg is cool with us sleeping over and a few of us just rack out right on the beach.

As I gaze at the waves lapping against the shoreline under the moonlit sky, I am placed in a peaceful trace. My mind turns to how much I have come to love this island over the last five years visiting LBI. I cherish every aspect of this coastal haven...the history of the island, the Jersey locals, the rhythmic tides, the fresh seafood, the whole enchilada.

The island was discovered by a Dutch explorer in 1614. Up until 1886, the only way to reach the island was by boat. That changed in 1886 when the first railroad bridge was constructed across the bay. With improved island access, grand hotels were established around the turn of the century with names such as Engelside, Parry House, Baldwin, Oceanic and Sunset. LBI became a hot spot for visitors from New York and Philadelphia. Many evenings I imagined myself being one of those early guests attending a Saturday night social, dancing on the massive wrap-around porch of the Victorian-styled Baldwin Hotel. It must have been a glorious experience. Sadly, it was a piece history that has been lost forever. All the original Victorian hotels as well as the railroad bridge were wooden structures destroyed by harrowing storms and fierce fires.

We made our own slice of history that summer with a couple of dozen Mules in Surf City. It was a kick-ass summer we would never forget.

Chapter Seventeen

"Two-a-days at the 'Berg"

Sunday afternoon, mid-August in Allentown, PA and sixty-five football players invade Benfer Hall on Muhlenberg College campus. Coach Balls is in the front hallway handing out room assignments. It has been the coach's custom to pair upper classmen with freshmen to help with their transition.

"Cobber, how the hell are you?" Coach Balls asks.

"Great Coach Sam. This summer with the guys at the Jersey Shore was a blast and we're in the best shape of our lives." I proudly reply.

Coach Sam barks, "We'll see about that. Tomorrow we conduct the fitness and conditioning tests bright and early 8:00 AM. That's where the bullshit stops and we'll see who did the work. You are rooming with Thomas Rex. He's a new kid to the program this year. Thomas transferred from the University of Pittsburgh. One thing led to the other and he left their program last year as a freshman. Thomas has tremendous size and he should be a good addition to the defensive line. I know you will make him feel part of the family. He's sitting in the lounge over on the left."

I look over and I'm amazed to see the size of Thomas when I exclaim, "Holy shit this guy is huge! What do you feed it?"

Thomas stands 6-foot-six and weighs around 285 pounds. That's huge for Division III football. On our entire roster we have only twelve players over 200 pounds.

"He's a bit shy. Go slow, Cobber." Coach Sam requests.

"It'll be fine Coach," I assure him.

Introducing myself I say, "Hey Thomas, I'm Jack Cobb but everybody calls me Cobber. We're gonna room together. Here's your key."

"Gee thanks," Thomas replies.

"Let's go up and get our stuff stowed away," I said.

Most of the rooms in Benfer Hall had bunk beds. Just as I had instructed Tank in our frat room last year, I told Thomas to take the bottom bunk. I did not want anyone his size hanging over me. After we got things placed in a somewhat organized fashion, I offer him a soda and ask him to take a seat. I want to engage him in a conversation to get to know him better. That's the best way I know to make someone feel more comfortable with his surroundings.

"Hey Thomas, from now on your nickname is gonna be T-Rex. It's a perfect fit since you are big as a dinosaur. You cool with that?" I inquire.

"Yeah, no problem. I went to high school right around here in Emmaus and that was my nickname there," T-Rex affirms.

"How come you transferred to Muhlenberg? I would think you would rather be playing with the Pittsburgh Panthers in front of 30,000 fans," I ask.

"To be honest, I was real homesick at first. At the time I still had a hometown girlfriend and being five hours away really played with my head. That started me thinking that Pittsburgh might not be such a good choice for me. But the final blow was realizing I did not have the speed for D-I ball. I was plenty big enough but I only ran a 5.6 forty time. Most all of the linemen were running near five-flat." T-Rex said.

"But why Muhlenberg?" I ask.

"Well...I grew up fifteen minutes from here and my dad started bringing me to games when I was only ten. I fell in love with the campus. But the most important factor was Muhlenberg's academic reputation. After undergraduate studies I hope to go to Med School. If you do well here there is a great chance to go that route," T-Rex replies.

"You got that right T-Rex. Muhlenberg places a ton of kids in medical and law schools. Well I for one am damn glad you chose the Mules. We're gonna turn this football program around this year and you've got the opportunity to be a big contributor. If you need any help with the transition, don't hesitate to get the skinny from me," I offer.

"Thanks Cobber, I appreciate that." T-Rex replies.

After thirty minutes of conversation I can sense T-Rex is much more at ease. I also suggest he think about joining ATO during the fall rush.

We go on to a team dinner that night together as the bonding continues. I made sure I got both of us in bed early because the fitness evaluations are tomorrow morning and it's important to show Coach Balls what we had accomplished this summer.

Our alarm abruptly breaks the silence at 6:30 AM but I've been semi-awake for the last hour with nervous excitement about the fit tests that will take place today. T-Rex, myself and the Palmisano twins eat a very light breakfast in anticipation of the mile run that's part of the battery of tests.

Before taking the field we have a team meeting in the stands with the coaches. Coach Marino lays out the goals and expectations for the upcoming season.

"Boys, let me make it clear that last year's one and eight season will not happen this year. We have the talent to be a factor in the MAC race. In addition to our twenty-five returning lettermen we have twenty freshmen and three transfers that give us added depth and will be strong contributors from the get-go. But talent only takes you so far. It will be our physical and mental preparation that differentiates us from other teams. We are going to ask more of you than you have ever been asked to do before as an athlete and as a student. We want to win at everything we do on the field, in the community and in the classroom. You are no good to the team if you fall down on your grades and become ineligible. If you need help with your coursework come to the coaches earlier rather than later. We have tutors that can assist you and get you back on track. We all need a little support now and then. Don't let pride or laziness get in the way of you getting the help you need.

We will be using the next three weeks to evaluate your individual strengths and development areas and determine where you can best contribute to the team. If you have concerns about where we have you playing or anything else, bring them directly to your assigned position coach or myself. We don't want distractions keeping us from our mission—of winning an MAC title. We will only realize that goal by sticking together as a family and outworking everybody on our schedule.

We have five weeks until our first game with Johns Hopkins and I assure you that we will be ready for the Blue Jays. We have scheduled two scrimmages in September with Albright and Wilkes Colleges. We are going to use those to make final determinations on the starting line-ups.

Your Captain, Jon Lambert has kept me abreast of all the strength and conditioning work you did in the summer. I am looking forward to seeing the results. Now let's get out there and warm-up. Coach Ballzano has your group assignments.

Remember gentlemen, our journey starts today and our destination is the MAC title. Now let me hear it...ONE, TWO, THREE, Mule Pride!" We all shout in unison following the coach's lead.

After about twenty-five minutes of light calisthenics and stretching exercises, we complete our warm-ups. At that point four stations have been set up that we rotate through in groups. After our Athletic Trainer, Dom "Band-Aid" Kitchline measures our height, weight and body fat percentage we perform a variety of physical tests to evaluate strength, muscular endurance, speed and flexibility. The last test is the one we all dread. It is a mile run around the track in the August heat.

I look over and see Sam Johnson standing on the sidelines. I couldn't help but think Sam should be out on the field sweating shoulder-to-shoulder with us but his tragic fall off the dormitory roof left him with restricted mobility and a pronounced limp. While playing was out of the question, Coach Marino talked Sam into serving as a student coach for the football program. That was a significant boost to the team to know that #60 would be with us on our journey.

I could tell the coaches were pleased with how our summer warriors performed in the conditioning tests. Personally I was very happy with ten percent body fat at one-hundred eighty-five pounds body weight but my forty time was a slow 5.1 seconds. I was blessed with endurance, but not speed. The other fitness evals showed my progress. In the 225 lb. bench press test I was able to do double the repetitions I did the previous year at 10 versus 5. But the real test was coming up with the mile run. The coaches divided us up into two groups. Guys over 200 lbs. and those under 200 lbs. The big boys went first. Their goal was to do the run in eight minutes or less and the smaller guys had to beat six minutes and forty-five seconds.

Most of us that were not running in the first group had our eyes fixed on Tank. We wanted him to do well. Last year Tank did the mile in something over nine minutes. We kept encouraging Tank to pace himself on each lap. He and T-Rex were the biggest guys on the track. After three quarters of a mile T-Rex had a little lead on Tank. T-Rex got to that marker in five minutes and fifty seconds while Tank made the three-quarter mark in six minutes and four seconds...just a little beyond the pace he needed to achieve eight minutes.

With all of us on the sidelines hooting and hollering, Tank began to pick up his pace and T-Rex started to fade. With half a lap to go Tank passed T-Rex and made his way to the back stretch. Amid chants of "Go Tank" and "Remember the Shore", #77 went past the finish line in seven minutes and fifty seconds. Not bad for a guy weighing two hundred and sixty-five pounds. T-Rex finished in a respectable eight minutes and five seconds. Again not too shabby for a man of his size.

The "small man race" was extremely competitive. Robbie Boll and Chet the Jet Stringer led from start to finish and blazed the course in five minutes and twenty seconds with The Jet taking the race by three strides. I beat my last year's time by almost a minute when I completed the course in six minutes and five seconds. I caught the Palmisano Twins on the last lap and dusted them off in the stretch. But the best part of it was that no one in either group tossed their cookies. Usually a few guys each year manage to blow lunch because they did not put in the conditioning work in the summer.

No vomiting signaled a good start to the season.

The Coaches gave us positive reinforcement for the overall showing of the team. They recognize that the summer workouts made a big difference and that we are starting at a much higher conditioning level this year compared to last year's preseason camp.

The first two weeks of football camp started before the rest of the students arrived on campus. While I miss seeing Debbie and my other friends, this is a perfect time to bond as a football team. The sixty-five of us along with the coaches are the only people around. We don't have distractions and the complete focus is on football. When school begins after Labor Day, the academic load will challenge our time management skills.

The initial two weeks of camp are especially tough on the freshman. For many it is their first extended time away from home without family and friends, and they go from being stars on their respective high school teams to trying to find a role as a Mule. Invariably each year we lose a couple guys to homesickness. This year is no different as two players dropped out the first week and returned home. But the biggest surprise to me was that one of the guys was a local kid from Bethlehem Catholic, the same school that Jim the Tasmanian Devil was from. The kid's home was no more than twenty minutes away and yet he walked off campus the second day.

Apparently the regimen and loneliness got to him. Our entire days are scheduled with practice in the morning and practice in the afternoon followed by position meetings at night. When you throw in the meals and sleep there is little time for anything else. That rigorous routine can overwhelm a kid just out of high school. The coaches and older players try to counsel the freshmen early in the preseason process, but despite our best efforts some attrition typically takes place.

My favorite part of the preseason camp is the first weekend. Because it's the first time the coaches give us downtime. We conducted an inter-squad scrimmage on Saturday morning and did not have anything scheduled except for a light, no-pads practice on Sunday afternoon. That gave us Saturday evening to do something fun.

We decide to go into town and take in a movie, American Graffiti, that was released last week. Just about everybody from the team went except for a few players that lived close and had dinner with family members. It was their loss because the camaraderie and companionship drew us even closer as a team.

Saturday evening was a cool contrast to the 85 degree afternoon so we make a decision to walk to the movie theater. The 30 minute walk gives us ample opportunity to talk in small groups about our shared experience; the sore muscles, the coaches' quirks, the gamey uniforms (only washed after the 2nd practice), etc. Walking in my small group are Chuck Biers, T-Rex, Tank, Jim Cahill, Frankie Johnson, Ron Wood and two freshmen; Jordan Mills and Stu Young.

"Hey Chuck, it feels good to be running with the first team doesn't it?" I ask Biers.

"Yeah, bro. It's our time. #62 and #72 gonna rock and block to the Championship." Chuck exclaims.

"There's a different feeling in camp. I can't put my finger on it but the pace of everything seems faster...the drills, the scrimmages, even the team meetings. This is my fourth year and there is definitely more excitement than in previous years," Jim Cahill adds.

"One thing that hasn't changed is the smell coming out of the drying room after two-a-days," says Frankie.

The drying room is where we hang up our uniforms and pads between practices to dry. The funny thing is that while the stark cement and block room filled with huge hangers smelled bad it somehow was an odor associated with football and that oddly evoked positive feelings for many of us.

"Yeah, that's some funky shit orbiting that spaceship," says Long Wood.

"I can't wait for the first scrimmage with Albright. It's bogus banging on our own dudes," Frankie adds.

"You got that right, Frankie. It's gonna be sweet kickin' some Lion ass. And I don't need no whip and chair to do my damage. I'm gonna tame those cats with these," Chuck declares as he flexes his biceps in the image of Arnold Schwarzenegger, the reigning Mr. Olympia.

"I can't believe the coaches didn't bust us for playing soap hockey in the shower. We coulda been in big fuckin' trouble if they caught us, " Jim Cahill states.

Occasionally to have some fun we would plug up the drains with towels and flood the shower room with about four inches of water. That provided the rink for our soap hockey game. Two teams slide around on their asses buck-naked trying to shoot a bar of soap into designated goals. It was the perfect way to decompress from a tough practice and raise our spirits. But the coaches frowned upon it and if we were caught it meant running laps. However, we had guards posted at every opening around the locker room to alert us of the coaches' movements. If a coach was spotted we could return the shower room to normal in a matter of seconds. Essentially we pulled the towels, stood-up and resumed washing our bodies. However the red chaffing on our asses from scooting around on our butts and the red marks on the parts of our bodies where the soap puck hit us were hard to explain.

"You fuckin' worry too much Cahill. Soap Hockey helps us blow off steam. All the rest of our time is scheduled to the goddamn minute. We need to have some fun once in a while!" Tank bellows.

"T-Rex, Jordan and Stu...you guys getting the hang of things?" I ask.

"Yeah it's a bit overwhelming at first. Not just the intensity of the practices, but even just dealing with a much larger playbook is tough," Stu answers.

"Trust me. After about three weeks everything will fall into place. You just need time to absorb all the new shit flowing in your head," Chuck explains.

"Stu, every player goes through that phase. It's not just you feeling this way. We all experienced that as freshmen. How about you big man? How you gettin' down with the Mule scene? " I ask T-Rex.

"I feel pretty good. My stint with The University of Pittsburgh prepared me for the college regimen, physically and mentally. So that stuff I feel comfortable with. It's just getting acclimated to new teammates and new coaches that will take a little time. I'm real happy with my decision to come here. But I have to tell you, my biggest surprise is finding out that the commitment required here at a Division III school is not that much different from a D-I." T-Rex divulges.

American Graffiti turned out to be a great movie. It had a ton of stars: Richard Dreyfuss, Ron Howard, Paul Le Mat, Harrison Ford, Cindy Williams, Wolfman Jack etc. The cool thing was that the entire series of vignettes takes place around one August night in 1962.

We all went bananas over the sexy blonde in the White T-bird. Later we learned the actress's name was Suzanne Somers. While she was definitely hot it was the 41 hit songs that played throughout the movie that made the biggest impact. We couldn't get them out of our heads. I'm sure the neighbors did not share our enthusiasm as we attempted to sing the Beach Boys' hit tune on the walk home at the top of our lungs.

> *Do you want to dance and hold my hand*
> *Tell me, baby, I'm your lover man*
> *Oh, baby, do you want to dance*
> *Do you want to dance under the moonlight*
> *Hold me, baby, all through the night*
> *Oh, baby, do you want to dance*
>
> *Do you, do you, do you*
> *Do you want to dance*
> *Do you, do you, do you*
> *Do you want to dance*
> *Do you, do you, do you, do you*
> *Do you want to dance*

Two weeks later we take a short bus ride to Reading, Pennsylvania. That's the site of our first scrimmage with the Albright Lions. I sit in the visitors' locker room going through my normal ritual. Every player possesses their individual way of preparing for a game. Being an intense guy it was easy for me to get myself psyched up for a fight. Therefore in the hours before a contest I try to relax and not waste a lot of nervous energy early. I want to peak emotionally right at the first kick-off. My pre-game focus centers on two things. Mentally going through the plays in my head and padding myself up to give me the feeling of invincibility.

It starts with getting my ankles taped. Then I slip on my pants that hold the hip and knee pads, followed by my shoulder pads and neck roll. Once my #62 jersey is pulled over my head the real craftsmanship begins. On each arm I pull into place two pieces of protective equipment; a one-piece forearm and elbow pad and a hand pad. Then with surgical precision I use white athletic tape to completely enshroud the pads. It takes one roll of tape for each arm. When finished, my arms are essentially war clubs. All that's visible are my fingers. And even sometimes with injuries those were taped together.

The last step in the process consists of putting on my helmet with a full-cage face mask. An opponent would more likely jam his fingers on my full-grill face mask than poke me in the eyes. With the helmet on, I pump it up to the right compression to fit snug and tight. I pride myself on sticking my face mask right into an opponent with my neck hyper-extended, the best way to prevent neck and spinal injuries.

Even though I weigh only one-hundred and eighty- five pounds, when fully cloaked in my armor I feel bulletproof.

My style of play developed out of necessity given my undersized stature. The two professional players that I model myself after are offensive guards, Conrad Dobler and Larry Little. The reasons for each are very different.

With Dobler of the St. Louis Cardinals, it's his nasty, physical style of play that intimidates opposing players. Sports Illustrated Magazine dubbed Dobler "Pro Football's Dirtiest Player". Quotes like the following solidified his image as a bad-ass, "I see defensive linemen jump to knock a pass down. When that happened near me, I'd smack'em in the solar plexus, and that got their hands down real quick." Dobler was dirty but he made his team better and rarely gave up any sacks.

With respect to Larry Little of the Miami Dolphins, I admire his quick pulling ability. He is a key contributor to the success of the Dolphins' punishing running attack and provides a lasting image seeing him lead Mercury Morris on a quick pitch to the outside. Even though Morris was lightening quick, Larry would always be out in front leading the way terrifying D-backs that attempted to stop the sweep. Larry Little, #66 was an integral part of last year's undefeated Super Bowl Champions. The only team in the 52 year history of the NFL to go undefeated in a season. I try my best to mimic Little's pulling techniques and quick feet. While I'm not the fleetest of foot in a race, I made myself an effective pulling guard by developing a quick first couple steps.

The Albright scrimmage went well. Each team was given twenty plays on offense and then rotated to defense on the next series. We continued that for about an hour and then each team was given the opportunity to practice a few punts, punt returns, kick-offs, kick returns and extra points. As is commonplace with scrimmages, no score was officially kept but all the players knew the results in their heads. Our first team offense scored four times while Albright's regulars scored twice. We had a lot of things to work on in the coming weeks but we were moving in a positive direction. There were still too many blown assignments and the coaches were quick to point that situation out.

On the bus ride home I felt my knee start to tighten up. It wasn't long before it swelled to double the size. Tank grabbed some ice from the trainer and helped me wrap the joint. I couldn't help but think the worst.

All my work over the summer is for nothing.

My emotions ranged from being pissed off to despair to denial.

"Tank, I can't believe this. The very first scrimmage and I hurt my knee. This is fuckin' ridiculous...I don't even remember getting hit there."

"Don't rush to any conclusions. It probably isn't serious. Just give it some time with the ice and elevation," Tank replies.

"This is bullshit. I don't know what I'll do if I can't play." I'm utterly drowning in self-pity.

From the front of the bus Don the Trainer shouts, "Cobb, keep your leg elevated until we get back home. Tank put this duffel bag under his leg. It will help keep the swelling down. I'll check the knee out when we get off the bus."

Forty minutes later I was laying on a training table at Muhlenberg with Don going through a number of manual manipulations to test the ligaments and joint stability.

"The knee seems to be stable but with all that swelling it is too hard to confirm how bad it is. I'm going to give you crutches because I don't want you to put any weight on it until you see our team doctor on Monday. Every hour ice the joint and keep it elevated the rest of the weekend." Don advised me.

Tank accompanied me as I struggled to adjust to walking with crutches. When we got to ATO all I wanted to do was hideout in my room and be away from everybody and everything. I don't want to talk about the knee.

I am not hurt. This is temporary. If I don't acknowledge it. It doesn't exist.

I didn't come out of my room on Sunday. I was determined to get the swelling down by totally immobilizing the knee. Tank got me a couple of fast food meals that I downed with a six pack of beer.

It was the second week of September so all the students were back on campus with classes in full swing. Debbie moved back into Benfer Hall after the football players transferred to their permanent residences. She came over to boost my spirits up, but I was acting like a butthole and not really receptive to her nurturing efforts.

"This is role reversal. Last semester you were cheering me up in the infirmary and now I have the opportunity to nurse you back to health," Debbie said with a smile on her face.

I was in no mood for small talk. "It's not that bad. You don't have to do anything." I replied stoically.

"Come on Jack, I can see you are hurting. Don't shut me out," Debbie said.

"I just really need to be by myself and rest. I don't feel like talking."

"Alright, you win. I'll leave you alone but call me if you start acting like a normal human being again."

I knew I was wrong, but I was feeling sorry for myself and I just wanted to drown my sorrows so I could get through the night and hear what the team doctor had to say on Monday.

My heart was racing pretty fast as I approached the training facility that morning. The team doctor was an older gentleman who had a local medical practice. He donated his time to the Muhlenberg athletic teams because he enjoyed being around college sports. He was a nice person, but I wasn't sure he had a medical specialty. I think he was a general practitioner.

Doc had me sit on the examination table as he went through similar manual manipulations that Don the

Trainer performed after the scrimmage. I couldn't wait for his prognosis.

"How did this happen, Jack?"

"I'm not sure. There was not one hit I remember. The knee just swelled up after the game. But it is much better now."

"There doesn't appear to be any serious ligament damage but we have to reduce the swelling around the joint. I am going to take a syringe and aspirate the fluid around the knee," Doc states.

The thought of a needle going in my knee scared the living shit out of me but at this point I'm open to anything that will help me get back on the field. Doc swabbed the swollen area with alcohol and then put some freezing gel around it for the stick. As he approaches me with the syringe I can't help but think it looks like a goddamn turkey baster.

"Holy shit Doc, is this gonna hurt a lot?" I ask.

"Not going to bother me much, Cobby," joked Doc.

Great my doctor thinks he's freaking Flip Wilson.

"Very funny, Doc," I remark with a sarcastic facial expression.

"You will feel it but the pain should be bearable. The key is to focus on how good you will feel afterwards. I want to warn you that I will need to manipulate the joint while I'm draining it so I get all of the excess fluid." Doc explains.

I'm trying to hide it from Doc but I'm petrified in my head. I don't like needles and I don't like doctors who think they are comedians but I'm attempting my best Clint Eastwood impression to put up a tough façade.

Once the Doc started the draining procedure the pain was terrible. He clearly understated how bad it would feel. I struggled to contain my discomfort during the two minute procedure as I contorted my face and made guttural sounds throughout. Doc pulled out two syringes of bloody-looking fluid during the process. He finished the entire procedure by injecting my knee with a cortisone shot. The cortisone ended up being a miracle medicine for me. Almost immediately the pain and swelling disappeared. By Wednesday, I was running plays without full contact and by the end of the week I was ready for the weekend scrimmage. My prayers had been answered and my season continued.

On Saturday, the Wilkes Colonials made the hour and ten minute bus ride from Wilkes-Barre, PA for our second and last scrimmage. For whatever the reason, the team was flat. Our performance lacked enthusiasm and our execution stunk. Coach Marino was clear about how he felt when he addressed us in the locker-room.

"We have exactly one week until we play Johns Hopkins. If we approach that game the way we did Wilkes today we will get our butts kicked. Our execution was poor. Our tackling and blocking were inconsistent. And making matters worse we played like we were sleepwalking...no passion....no energy! Hopkins will embarrass us if we don't raise our game!" He slammed his clipboard on the ground and his yelling worsened.

"I don't care if we had one more score than the Colonials today. We should have pushed them all over the field. I want each one of you to go back and reflect on your performance today. Think about what you could have done better and think about how you can make the players around you better. We have to focus as a team on our game plan but that starts with each one of you executing your role exceptionally. Each one of you has to win his individual battle if the team is to win the game. I want no excuses this week. Get your minds on what you need to do. Tomorrow we meet in the team room at 2:00 PM sharp to look at the film. We also will be communicating the two-deep roster and starters for Hopkins. Now get some rest and be ready to work hard."

The Coach's words had the appropriate effect. After self-reflection, we renewed our commitment to executional excellence and had a strong week of practice.

I was pleased when the line-up was posted because it confirmed that I was starting at left guard next to Tank (#77) the left tackle, while Chuck (#72) was starting at the right guard slot alongside Charlie Driscoll (#67). Jorge Mendoza (#51) rounded out the offensive line at center.

Thursday of game week came around and two significant events happened. After practice we learned that Jim Croce, one of my favorite singer/songwriters from South Philly was killed in a tragic plane crash. Only thirty years of age he was travelling from Louisiana to a gig in Texas when his plane crashed after take-off. I loved his song lyrics and immediately my mind went straight to his song "The Hard Way Every Time".

>Yeah, I've had my share of broken dreams
>And more than a couple of falls

And in chasin' what I thought were
moonbeams
I have run into a couple of walls
But in looking back at the places I've been
The changes that I've left behind
I just look at myself to find
I've learned the hard way every time

*Croce must have known me when he wrote this
song. I seem to have to learn the hard way too.*

That evening a number of us ran back to the frat house in anticipation of the televised Battle of the Sexes. About thirty ATO brothers crammed into our living room and watched along with 90 million worldwide television viewers as Billie Jean King, one of the top female tennis players in the world entered the Houston Astrodome in Cleopatra style. She was propped up by four bare-chested muscle men dressed as Roman slaves. Bobby Riggs, a 55 year old former tennis pro followed in a rickshaw drawn by a bevy of gorgeous models wearing skimpy outfits. The atmosphere as reported by ABC was electric. The largest crowd (30,472) ever to view a tennis match was divided along gender lines. Promoters hyped the angle, male chauvinists versus the women-libbers. Riggs presented King with a giant lollipop and she gave him a piglet.

Once the match began the competition turned out to be somewhat anticlimactic. King, 26 years younger than Riggs, ran Bobbie all over the court and easily defeated the elder statesman 6-4.

The Jet and I won a lot of bets from our ATO brothers since they firmly believed that Riggs was going to repeat the success he had against Margaret Court, a great Australian player this past May when he defeated her 6-2, 6-1 using drop shots and lobs.

The real lesson had little to do with gender. It was all about the competitor that executes his or her game plan flawlessly, with focus and energy is going to win the contest. That was the mental framework the Mules needed to display against Johns Hopkins.

Chapter Eighteen

"The Baltimore Beginning"

It is Saturday morning. This is what we've been waiting for almost a year. What we worked for so hard for in the summer. Today is the first game of the 1973 Football season against Johns Hopkins, located in Baltimore, Maryland. We lost to the Blue Jays last year by a score of 17-9. After a team breakfast we board a bus for the two hour ride.

Frankie Johnson has a Sears Portable 8-Track Player with him on the trip so we can relax to music. Nothing like a little R & B with the Spinners' I'll Be Around...

> "This is our fork on the road
> Love's last episode
> There's nowhere to go, oh, no
>
> You made your choice
> Now it's up to me to bow out gracefully
> Though you hold the key, but baby
>
> Whenever you call me, I'll be there
> Whenever you want me, I'll be there
> Whenever you need me, I'll be there
> ***I'll be around...***"

"Hey Cobber, if you need me today just call me, (sung along with the music playing) *I'll be around*. If you have trouble blocking your Blue Jay I'll be there for you," Tank sings.

"Kiss my ruby red ass, you jive turkey," I shoot back.

"Well, excusssse ME!" Tank wisecracks sarcastically imitating Comedian Steve Martin.

"Kids, play nice and feel da funk," Frankie intervenes.

"You're right Frankie. We gotta focus on plucking some Blue Jays." Chet the Jet adds.

We arrive safely and begin our individual rituals in the visitors dressing room. I am padding and taping my arms to perfection. Paul is stroking his lucky T-shirt. Frankie is listening to music with headphones. Everyone has their ceremonial habits.

The locker room atmosphere is building to a crescendo of excitement and just before we take the field for warm-ups Coach Marino brings us to a fever pitch with a motivational pep talk.

"Bring it in, gentlemen. We put in the work. Not only in summer camp but the entire off-season. We stand here today, better conditioned, better prepared, and more committed than our opponents. Now it is time to show it on the field. The difference will be our flawless execution. They can't match our energy and eventually we will force them into mistakes. They will not be able to stay with us for four quarters. We will impose our will on them. Today we regain Mule PRIDE!"

We circle around Coach. "Hands in...one, two, three, **MULE PRIDE**!" We scream in unison.

From the opening kick-off, the new Mules strutted our stuff. We rolled out our new offensive scheme, the Veer Option invented by Bill Yeoman, Coach of the University of Houston Cougars in 1965. The Veer offense depends on speed and has been very useful when small, skilled teams go up against larger clubs, which in our case is every week. The Veer is all about creating angles for the quarterback and the running backs. The quarterback has the critical job of reading how the defense is reacting and execute one of three options: hand the football to the fullback on the dive play, keep the ball and run to the outside or pitch the ball to a running back.

Only one freshman made the starting lineup. That was Jordan Mills (#32) at halfback and he made an immediate impact. His nickname is the Hammer because at 5'9" and 210 lbs. he runs with exceptional power. Against Hopkins, Jordan rushed for 201 yards on 27 carries while Ron Wood (#42) at fullback gained 110 yards on 23 carries. Overall we amassed 373 yards via the ground, trouncing the Blue Jays 35 – 6 with Arnie running the offense brilliantly. The Mules made a resounding statement and gave notice that we would be a factor in the MAC title race.

The only thing that spoiled the day for me was an incident that took place in the fourth quarter when the game was firmly in Muhlenberg's control. The opposing tackle I had been going up against all day who outweighed me by a good fifty pounds was getting very frustrated because his team was losing. In our offense, I don't have to drive my opponent away from his starting position. I just have to neutralize him and create a channel for our backs to run through. My responsibility is to do anything within reason to tie up my adversary. With about five minutes left in the game I crab block my opponent for what was probably the twentieth time in the game. I'm on all fours driving my body into his legs. Finally out of total frustration he starts pounding on my back with his hands clasped together while he stood directly over me. Not stopping there, he pulls off his helmet and begins beating me on the back with it. Now I'm okay with him beating on my back with his hands because if he's doing that, he isn't making tackles. But when he took off his helmet and beat me with it that really pissed me off. I literally exploded to my feet and drove the point of my elbow into his neck. As luck would have it the head official caught me retaliating against this whack job and tossed me out of the game. My only consolation was that my rival was going to be eating soft foods for a while.

What a dubious distinction. The only record I would ever hold at Muhlenberg College was getting ejected from two consecutive football games. Coach Sam shared a few choice words with me and I made a commitment to myself right then and there to never let my temper get the best of me again.

Chapter Nineteen

Home crowds – home cooking"

Up next is a home game with Delaware Valley College from New Britain, PA. The Rams beat us last year 35-14 and we are looking for redemption.

I loved home games because my parents were able to attend and afterwards we had a ritual of going out to eat at either the King George Inn, a historic stone roadhouse built in 1756, or The Village Inn on Tilghman Street. Usually a few other Mule families would come along as well. There was nothing better than to kick back after a game with the 3-Fs; food, family and fun. On occasion my sister would join us when her schedule permitted.

As the Del Val players exited their bus, we could see they possessed a tremendous size advantage over us. That size supremacy made it difficult for us to get our ground game going in the first quarter. But with the Rams focusing all their attention on stopping our running game, the passing game emerged. With one minute elapsed in the second quarter, Arnie hits Robbie Boll streaking down the left sideline with a 65-yard touchdown pass. Arnie follows that up in the next series with a 45-yard touchdown strike to Chet The Jet on a post pattern down the middle of the field. By halftime we were leading 21-0 and the game is well in hand.

Our physical conditioning wears the opposition down. It was a warm day for the end of September and the Rams' tongues are hanging out. We did a complete reversal of last year's score by beating Del Val to the tune of 35-14.

Robbie ended up catching 3 passes for 160 yards and two touchdowns. Arnie was 15 of 25 passing attempts for 276 yards. Frankie was a monster on defense with two sacks and five tackles. It was a complete victory in all phases of the game.

What happened in our third week was unexpected. We travelled to Annville, PA in the middle of Pennsylvania Dutch country to play Lebanon Valley College. The Flying Dutchman were not highly regarded but played exceptional defense that day and the game ended up in a 7-7 tie. The bus drive home seemed a lot longer than the hour and twenty minutes it actually took.

"Boys, today we did it to ourselves. Not taking anything away from Lebanon Valley but our execution did us in. We had twelve penalties that cost us over 100 yards and stopped four of our drives cold. The positive is that we are still undefeated in the MAC but we have to regain our edge. Football is as much mental as is it physical. We need to eliminate the mental mistakes next week against Ursinus and we will be fine. We got through the game without injuries so that's a positive. Be ready to work on Monday after film session," said Coach Marino.

The Lebanon Valley game was a wake-up call. We used it as a learning experience and the following week we beat up on the Ursinus Bears in Collegeville, PA 31 – 14. The running game was effective as we outrushed the Bears 205 yards to 67 yards. Our record stood at 3-0-1 with Homecoming up next on the schedule.

Homecoming week was usually filled with distractions and this one was no different. One issue confronting me was who was going to accompany Debbie during the halftime ceremony when the Homecoming Court is announced. She gave me a list of acceptable escorts among my friends. I decided to approach Wolfman.

"Greg, I have a favor to ask you man," I said.

"What is it?" Greg replied.

"Well Debbie is part of the Homecoming Court and she needs an escort during halftime of the game. Would you do it for me?" I asked.

"Cobber, Cobber, Cobber. No problem. Let's face it. Deb's gonna get a big upgrade when she latches on to my arm," Greg responded with pride.

"Yeah you're a real Elvis look-a-like, Wolfman," I said sarcastically.

"What should I do if Debbie can't control herself and starts making out with me on the fifty-yard line, jamming her tongue down my throat?" Greg joked with a grin.

"I don't have to worry about that. Gigi will cut off your exceptionally small dick if she catches you kissing another woman," I reassure him.

"Hey I am master of my domain...king of my castle," Greg said.

"You talk big when Gigi is in another state. But I do thank you for helping out. I'll let Debbie know you're happy to do it." I said.

In addition to my parents and sister, I have two aunts and uncles who plan on attending the game. They live in

Maryland and are quite the characters. They knew how to have fun in any situation.

The game against the Dickenson Red Devils from Carlisle, PA is tightly fought throughout the contest. Neither club gets up by more than seven points. We scored in the first quarter with a strong running attack as Jim Cahill (#33) ran through three tacklers on his way to the end zone from seven yards out. Dickenson replied with a defensive touchdown as Arnie's screen pass was intercepted by the Red Devil's left cornerback as he jumped our receiver's route and sprinted in for a touchdown from our 37-yard line.

Coach Balls went ballistic as he yelled, "Goddamn it Palmisano! If it isn't there, don't force it! And you guys on the O-line...put their asses on the ground. If you had blocked it the way we drew it up that son-of-bitch wouldn't have blown up the play! You're walking around with your heads up your asses. Get in the game!"

We took Coach's encouragement and went on a long touchdown drive with Arnie finishing it off with a 15-yard touchdown pass in the right corner of the end zone on a jump ball pass to his brother (#24) at tight end. That is how the first half finished with the Mules taking a tenuous 14-7 lead.

While the football team was enduring the coaches' colorful feedback in our locker room, the Homecoming festivities were taking place. Debbie had to do double duty as a sideline 'Berg cheerleader and a member of the Homecoming Court. After the Pom-Pom squad performed its routine, the Homecoming royalty was announced. One by one the couples were introduced to the crowd.

"From Upper Saddle River, New Jersey...sophomore Debra D'Angelo accompanied by senior Greg Wolfe," the announcer declared. Debbie was a good three inches taller than Wolfman who was wearing a checkered sport coat. The boys from ATO could not miss the opportunity to heckle Wolfman. And in full voice they shouted random taunts,

> "Hey look its Cher and Sonny Boner!"
>
> "No it's Quasimodo and Esmeralda!"
>
> "Why does Debbie have her Cocker Spaniel with her? No animals allowed on the field!"
>
> "Hey Wolfman, she's gotta body that won't quick and you've gotta brain that won't start!"

To Greg's credit he took the verbal slaps undeterred. With a broad smile and confident gait he had the air of Reggie Jackson striding to home plate as he ushered Debbie arm-in-arm to mid-field. Squarely situated on the fifty-yard line, Wolfman took a bow as the couple assumed its place in the lineup.

With the halftime festivities completed, the second half began. The third quarter was a battle between the defenses. With three minutes left in the quarter, the Dickenson QB threw a 5-yard screen pass and his halfback turned it into a 48-yard touchdown that tied the game 14-14. At the start of the 4th quarter, the Mules responded with a long drive that began on our own twenty-five yard line. Other than one pass completion to Chet the Jet for 13 yards, our offense dominated via our running game. Mills and Wood took turns churning out the yardage. With the ball resting on the Red Devils' 8-yard line, we called a naked bootleg. The play began with virtually the entire offense running to the right side showing a sweep to the halfback. Because of the previous running success, the Dickenson defense jumped all over the play fake. Even the left defensive end that was supposed to stay at home and protect his end of the field got caught inside as Arnie pulled back the ball and reversed his direction for a touchdown and a 21 – 14 lead.

Holding on to a slim 7-point lead late in the 4th quarter Arnie was blind-sided and fumbled the ball on our on twenty-yard line. Capitalizing on the Mule mistake, the Red Devils marched the ball into the end zone. With the score at 21-20, Dickenson lined up for the extra point to tie the game. T-Rex made the play of the game when he broke through the middle of the line of scrimmage and blocked the PAT. We mobbed T-Rex as he ran off the field.

After our big break we ran out the play clock making two first downs with our running attack to win the game 21-20. It felt good to win our Homecoming Game but we all knew we had made it way too close.

Before going home my Dad wanted to show our relatives from Maryland a frat party. ATO had organized a party with a "Mobster theme". Partygoers were encouraged to dress up like gangsters and we had an old bathtub full of grain alcohol and punch. Needless to say my crazy aunts and uncles had a great time.

With the DJ playing Listen to the Music by the Dobbie Brothers, our pledges burst in and pretended to shoot up the house like the St. Valentine's Day Massacre.

> "Don't you feel it growin', I say, day by day
> People gettin' ready for the news
> Some are happy, some are sad
> Well now Mama gonna let the music play
>
> What the people need love, is a way to make them smile
> Ain't so hard to do if you know how
> Gotta get a message, get it on through
> Oh now Mama gonna get that after a while
>
> Oh, listen to the music
> Oh, listen to the music
> Oh, listen to the music
> All the time
> Yeah, ooh"

Aunt Rose grabbed one of the toy guns and with a smile on her face shot back at the intruders. She was not going down easy without a fight. Shortly afterwards we had to stop Aunt Jess from jumping into the bathtub gin. Fortunately for the fraternity, my family had to leave early to make the drive home. If they had stayed until the end the aunts would have been drinking us under the table.

The Dickenson game was much too close for comfort. So the coaches had us do live intra-squad scrimmaging on Tuesday and Wednesday to raise the intensity and focus on execution. The practice tactics were very effective. The next week we travelled just outside Philadelphia to take on the Little Quakers of Swarthmore College. The tone was set from the beginning as Swarthmore won the coin toss and elected to kick-off to us. Chet the Jet returned it to the Mule 40-yard line. The first play Arnie faked a hand-off and the Little Quakers jumped all over it. Then he threw deep to Robbie Boll for a 60-yard touchdown. From that point on, we never looked back. We had over 460 yards of total offense and beat Swarthmore 51 – 0. It made for a short bus ride home.

Chapter Twenty

"The Hot Dog gets ground-up"

We've been waiting for November 3rd since the football schedule was announced last year. That is the day Widener College is scheduled to invade Muhlenberg Stadium. Last year they embarrassed us 48-2. Billy "White Shoes" Johnson, one of the best college football players at any level, scored 5 touchdowns on us as he ran for 224 yards. For his success against the Mules he was featured in Sports Illustrated's Faces in the Crowd and was quoted, "Today I felt so good I could score on the Dallas Cowboys."

Known as the ultimate hot dog, Billy was famous for his white shoes when most players wore black, and his colorful, exuberant end zone dances. As an example of his cocky antics, he ran the last ten yards of his 4th touchdown against us backwards as he taunted defenders extending his arm out with the ball...the final insult.

We could not wait to get a second shot at Widener's prize running back who was also a 9.5 sprinter on their track team. This year they come into the game with a perfect 5-0 record and have just laid a 54-0 whopping on the Ursinus Bears. The Pioneers are ranked second in the voting for the Lambert Bowl, representing the best Division III football team in the east. The Mules own a 5-0-1 record and are ranked 7th in the Lambert poll.

We are fully aware we have to do two things very well if we are to win the game. First, we need to run the ball effectively and dominate time of possession so we don't give White Shoes a lot of opportunities on offense. Last year he rushed for 1556 yards, scored 27 touchdowns and is on the same pace this year.

Second, our defense needs to contain Billy when Widener does have the ball. It was understood that he would invariably gain yardage but we had to eliminate the long touchdown runs. We must make White Shoes work for every yard he gains today. The average length of his rushing touchdowns is 36 yards for the year! We have to contain his explosive plays.

As I dress for the game I can't help but feel my emotions taking over. We were embarrassed last year. And now we have the opportunity to get back at the Pioneers in what is the most hyped game I've ever been a part of. It has all the ingredients, two unbeaten teams and the best running back in Division III football, maybe the best in all of college football.

Coach Marino walks in and reinforces what we need to do, "Gentlemen, this is not going to be a long speech. Most of you were at the Widener Stadium last year. Remember how it felt walking off the field that day. Remember their end zone dances. Remember the score. 48 to 2. And the taunting. This year we get back Mule Pride. We will not be denied. The offense is going to control the line of scrimmage and the defense is going to put eleven bodies on White Shoes every time he gets the ball. We are going to make him earn every yard he gets. We put in the work, now let's execute our plan. Bring it in...One...Two...Three...MULE PRIDE!"

The atmosphere is amazing. Over 5,000 fans are stuffed in Muhlenberg Stadium that has a capacity of 3,000. Those fans not seated in the stands completely encircle the field standing on the running track. It is a perfect fall day for football, sunny and in the high 50's.

We have our running game working effectively. Early in the first quarter, we march the ball 71 yards for a touchdown capped off by Arnie Palmisano's 10-yard run. The Pioneers take advantage of a blocked punt and White Shoes scores from twenty yards out and finishes it off with his knee-knocking, ball-waving, touchdown dance. The first quarter ends 7-7.

In the second quarter the Pioneers take advantage of another Mule mistake. We fumble on our own 27-yard line. Widener recovers the ball and uses six plays capped off by a 1-yard quarterback sneak to take a 13-7 lead. T-Rex blocked their extra point attempt and the score remains 13-7 as the half ends.

As we settle into the locker room at the half-time break Captain Jon Lambert gathers us around the chalkboard and reminds us what needs to be done,

"Guys, we worked too hard in the summer and this season to fall short now. The only reason Widener has any points at all is our mistakes. We have to protect the ball. Suck it up and let's finish these guys off. We are winning the battles at the line of scrimmage. Now let's turn that butt-whipping into points. Think about how it is going to feel when we walk off that field today winners. Nothing is going to stop us. We need to do it for the coaches...for the school...but most of all for each other. Now let's kick ass! Mule Pride!"

Jon's pep talk raises the team's emotions. Despite being down by six points, you can feel the air of confidence within the clubhouse. Once we get back out on the field Chuck Biers and I perform our weekly ritual of butting heads against each other. People give us strange looks as we thud our foreheads as hard as we can into each other and scream out,

"Ahhhh...Pioneers going down Ahhhh...Pioneers going down...Ahhhhh....PIONEERS GOING DOWN!"

> *Our brains are probably going to pay for those head butts in the future but for now it seems like the right thing to do.*

We make an immediate statement at the beginning of the 3rd quarter by putting together a 48-yard drive marked by a strong running attack. With the ball on our 7-yard line, Arnie calls a trap option up the middle. I love that play because I get to pull from the left side and hit the first thing I see on the right side. Jorge Mendoza (#55) hikes the ball and slant blocks the guy over me. Chuck Biers (#72) ignores the defensive player situated over him and angles left to block the middle linebacker. I pull and step quickly to the right and explode on Chuck's guy who fails to recognize the trap. I drive him to the ground before he knows where I came from. Arnie hands off the ball to Ron Wood who follows Chuck up the middle for a touchdown. With a successful extra point the Mules lead 14-13.

Before the third quarter was over, disaster struck again for the Mules as Arnie fumbled on our own 22-yard line. White Shoes gains 7 yards on his first carry and then blasts around left end for a 15-yard touchdown punctuated with his TD shimmy. Widener then lines up for a two-point conversion. Frankie Johnson (#64) and Jon Lambert (#52) combine to stuff the QB on an option play. With the missed conversion the Pioneers lead 19-14 going into the 4th quarter.

In the middle of the 4th quarter, Coach Balls sequesters the entire first team offense around the bench and makes it clear what we need to do.

"This is it. This is the drive. The defense will get us the ball back but then it's up to you. Look at each other...commit to each other. No mistakes. We drive the ball down their goddamn throats. This is payback time."

We proceed to do Coach Balls' bidding. We instigate a fifteen-play drive to move 77 yards to the Pioneers' 2-yard line. There the emotional roller coaster hits a low point as we are stopped one foot short of a first down. The Pioneers take over deep in their territory. However two plays later our middle linebacker, Jon Lambert cracks White Shoes and Billy coughs up the ball as defensive end Tommie Smits (#70) makes the recovery on the 5-yard line. But the Pioneer defense stiffens and three cracks at right tackle only get us to the 3-yard line. On fourth down Arnie attempts a pass to Robbie Boll but the split end is shoved illegally and the Mules receive the ball on the one-yard line. From there Arnie sneaks it in off the left side. With a successful extra point the Mules lead 22-19. However with two minutes left there is still angst amongst the crowd that White Shoes might perform his magic with a game-ending dash.

The Pioneers return the kick-off to the 24-yard line. A complete pass moves the ball to the 34-yard line. But after 3 unsuccessful pass attempts, the Pioneer QB tries to cross-up the Mule defense by giving the ball to Johnson for a sweep of the left end, but the Pioneer speedster is swarmed under. As the game clock counts down to zero the entire Muhlenberg bench erupts into impromptu Hot Dog dances. To his credit, Billy Johnson took it in stride as the field is stormed by the crowd and hundreds are imitating his touchdown gyrations all around him. White Shoes just smiles and accepts the taunts without incident. I respect Billy Johnson for his ability to take crap as well as he could give it out.

That Saturday White Shoes got to do his hot dog dance twice while Muhlenberg got to do it just once but boy was that one opportunity sweet. Johnson did end up with 101 yards on 17 carries and two touchdowns but the Mule defense accomplished what it set out to do— keep him contained and avoid big yardage plays. The Mules amassed 236 yards rushing with Wood getting 90-yards and Mills getting 76-yards. This was complete vindication for last year.

With the win the Mules improved to a record of 6-0-1 and third place in the Lambert Bowl voting. The parties on campus lasted all night. Most of us spent the night at Lambda Chi since ATO was not scheduled for a party that evening. Debbie and Scott "Prize Hog" Cressman had to walk me home to the frat and roll me in bed. A whole lot of pent-up emotions were released that night with the help of two friends, Bud and Boone's Farm.

Chapter Twenty-one

"Diplomatic Disaster"

The Franklin and Marshall Diplomats are next up on the schedule. The only blemish on their record is a 21-20 loss to Widener College. While I don't want to admit it, the Widener victory has been tough to put behind us. We are going through the process of studying and preparing for the Diplomats but emotionally many of us are still riding that high from upending the Pioneers the previous week.

The one hour and twenty minute bus ride to Lancaster, PA to face F & M is quieter than usual. I can't put my finger on it, but it feels like something is missing. Whether it is the pressure of making good on our promise to Sam Johnson of winning the MAC title, or the fact that we have lost to F & M the last two years, there is noticeable tension among the players. It is not anything spoken but rather clenched jaws and uneasy quiet that reveals the underlying strain.

To conserve my energy, I close my eyes and turn my thoughts to the Jersey Shore. Last summer was the epitome of working hard and playing hard. The esprit de corps among the twenty-five of us was as strong as I have ever felt. The togetherness was genuine. We truly cared about each other's welfare as we tied our individual fortunes to the goals of the collective group. Envisioning white-tipped waves lapping against a white, sandy beach, the sun's rays against my cheeks and the scent of ocean saltwater, my nerves are calmed momentarily.

Once the game starts, it doesn't take long for misfortune to hit the Mules. On a third down pass play with ten minutes left in the first quarter, the F & M outside right linebacker blitzes Arnie from the blindside and with a violent tackle knocks him to the ground. It is evident that Arnie is seriously hurt. As he is helped off the field in a stretcher we can see his eyes, swollen and red with disappointment.

"Get those bastards back for me, Cobber," Arnie says under his breath, fighting back the pain of a suspected cracked rib.

"We'll do our best. You just focus on taking care of yourself, Meatball," I reply.

That would be the last play Arnie would be involved in for the remainder of the year. With our offensive leader fallen, we struggle to execute our game plan.

The Diplomats scored 21 unanswered points before we scored in the third quarter on a Mills touchdown. The game finishes with F & M securing a 28-7 win and the MAC title.

No one was in the mood for any parties after the Diplomat debacle. Several of us gather at the ATO frat house on Saturday night to watch a little TV, down a few beers but most of all to console each other. We have to regroup and try to understand what went wrong and work through it.

Playing on CBS is the Saturday Night Comedy line-up: All in the Family, M*A*S*H, The Mary Tyler Moore Show, The Bob Newhart Show and the Carol Burnett Show. We weren't really watching the TV as it plays in the background.

"We blew it. We fucking lost our chance at the conference championship," Tank utters with disgust.

"I'm so pissed we let down. We played flat and just plain sucked!" Paul declares as he slams his fist into the couch he's sitting on.

"Yeah and we didn't make our commitment to you," Chet says as he looks towards Sam Johnson.

"Don't worry 'bout me, Bro. There is still work to be done. Do it for yourselves," Sam insists.

"Sam's right. Our biggest rival is left and the Greyhounds have beaten us 8 years in a row. That's "re-god-damn-diculous," I announce.

"Finishing seven, one and one is a hell-of-a lot better than going six, two and one." Chet add.

Robbie Boll diverts our attention back to the television when he injects, "Hey look at that Miller Light commercial. That's fucking hilarious with Bubba Smith and Dick Butkus." He is referring to a new commercial that has the two great pro football players arguing the eternal debate of which is better about the beer, "Tastes Great or Less Filling." Once it ends we return to our conversation.

"Arnie, how are you feeling?" Ron asks.

"Not too bad. I didn't fracture the ribs but I did tear the cartilage between the ribs. The doc says I need to limit my activity for 12 weeks. He gave me some anti-inflammatory drugs and this ace bandage," Arnie replies lifting his shirt up to display the ace wrap. "It's pretty tough breathing."

"That's a shame you are going to miss the Moravian game," Ron counters.

"Fire Hose will do well. He's ready," Arnie says referring to Rick Mason, the back-up QB.

"It's gonna be our job to make him successful by blocking our asses off," Chuck adds emphatically.

"This is my last chance at the Greyhounds. I have lost to those bastards every year. I don't intend to make it four-in-a-row," Jim Cahill declares.

"We got your back, Jimbo," Frankie responds as he slaps Cahill between the shoulder blades.

A cold front moves in just before the traditional game with Moravian. We wake up that Saturday to temperatures not much above freezing and it isn't supposed to get much warmer by kick-off. Due to the expected cold, I add a thermal shirt under my uniform.

Coach Marino is crystal clear with his instructions as he corrals us in a small area adjacent to the lockers to deliver his pre-game talk. The entire team is literally on top of each other.

"Gentlemen, do you know the significance of the year 1964?" A long pause ensues as Coach looks around the room.

"That was the last time we beat the Greyhounds. We have lost to Moravian EIGHT YEARS IN A ROW. That's long enough. We exercised a lot of demons when we beat the Pioneers and White Shoes, but this is the most important game we play every year. Throw out the damn records. They don't mean anything. This one game makes a team's season if you win it. When you take the field today block out everything...the crowd...the cold...the past. Concentrate on one thing...PHYISICALLY IMPOSING YOUR WILL on the guy across from you. We will win this game at the POINT OF ATTACK."

Coach is so amped up as he's speaking he head-butts the locker next to him creating a gash on his forehead. Blood starts to trickle down his face. "We are FIGHTING FOR OUR PRIDE. When you block out there...put your guy ON THE GROUND! When you tackle...put your head THROUGH HIS CHEST! Eight years of defeats leaves a real bad taste. Today we start our win streak. No mistakes. No regrets. Bring it in! ONE, TWO, THREE, MULE PRIDE!"

At this point one of the assistant coaches makes a futile attempt to place a towel on Coach Marino's head to stop the bleeding. Coach shoves the towel away and then slaps each one of us on the shoulder pads as we run out of the locker room. With the mental image of blood flowing down the bridge of our rabid Coach's nose, we storm the field psyched out of our minds. Chuck and I perform our pre-game ritual with more frenzy than ever before. We head-butt each other with complete abandon like two territorial mountain goats.

Muhlenberg Stadium is overflowing with 4,200 excited fans and they sense a change of history. Playing with great emotion, the Mules take command of the game by out-rushing our traditional rivals two-to-one. We score twice in the first half. One on a sustained drive while the second was a short sideline pass from Rick Fire Hose Mason to Paul Palmisano that Paul ran in for a fifty-yard touchdown. We lead 14-0 lead at the half.

The second half begins with the Moravian QB tossing a 54-yard touchdown that surprises our secondary. The game is won in the third quarter when T-Rex causes a fumble at our 2-yard line just as the Greyhounds are getting ready to score. Frustrated by the mistake, a Moravian lineman attacks T-Rex and receives a 15-yard personal foul. That brings the ball out to the 17-yard line and gives us breathing room. From there our offensive line and running backs Wood and Mills take over. In dominant fashion, we drive the ball 83 yards using 12 running plays to score our third touchdown. Mills finishes the drive with a slashing run from the 6-yard line. With that statement drive Muhlenberg leads 21-7. Moravian would score late in the game but the home crowd erupts as eight years of frustration come to an exhilarating end with a 21-13 victory.

Our overall record improved to 7-1-1 and we end up 10th in the Lambert Bowl voting but we fall short of our goal to win the MAC title. Had we won the championship, we might have been in contention for selection to the Division III NCAA playoffs. We learn later that Juniata, Bridgeport, Wittenberg and San Diego are selected to compete for the national D-III title. The semi-finals will be played on December 1st with the finals scheduled for December 8th. It appears that our season is over with the triumph against our arch-rival, but we learn of an exciting opportunity the next day.

Chapter Twenty-two

"Thriller at the Chiller"

Coach Marino calls a meeting in the Student Union the day after the Moravian game. We all thought it was going to be a rehash of the season along with getting the underclassman to begin thinking about next year, but we are caught off-guard with the Coach's message.

"Guys we have a unique opportunity in front of us. A former high school teammate and life-long friend, Jay Lamb, is currently the Vice President of Sales & Marketing for Thermo King Corporation in Minnesota. For the past week he has been talking with me about promoting a bowl game between two D-III football teams. Jay played college ball at the University of St. Thomas in Minneapolis and is a passionate alum. The Tommies finished this season at 9 and 1 and ended up second in their conference. He thought it would be a great idea to pit our team against St. Thomas," Coach Marino announces.

As soon as the words get out of Coach's mouth, a buzz of excitement goes through the room. We are ecstatic about the potential opportunity to keep playing football.

"Before you get too excited, you need to know about the cost. Thermo King Corporation is going to be the corporate sponsor and will provide funds for things like stadium rental, promotional ads, referees, etc. However we would be responsible for a portion of the travel costs. That is estimated to be $400 per player. I had a preliminary discussion with our Chancellor and he said the school could come up with half of that amount but since it was not budgeted for the players would need to come up with $200 on their own. I would like to take a vote on whether to go or not, and remember a yes vote means you will contribute $200 to the trip. The target date for the bowl game is Saturday, December 8th. That only gives you a few weeks to find the money," Coach adds.

Collectively every member of the team expresses the following sentiment, "No sweat Coach. We'll get the dough. One way or the other."

"Coach, where will the game be played? Will we have to play the game at the University of St. Thomas's field?" Captain Jon Lambert asks.

"No, I asked for a neutral site and my buddy wants to make it a bigger event so he has already reached out to the University of Minnesota. Their last home game is against Wisconsin next Saturday so their stadium is available. It has an artificial surface called tartan turf so even with bad weather the field should be serviceable. Memorial stadium seats 56,000 but Jay is targeting a crowd attendance of ten to fifteen thousand. He is going to promote the game among Thermo King's dealer network and encourage their participation," Coach replies.

"All in favor, raise your hand," Captain Jon challenges us.

Every arm in the conference room goes up in unison.

"Ok, men. I will let Jay know that he has a game," Coach Marino states emphatically.

"Coach, what's the name of the Bowl Game?" Tank asks.

"Well, Thermo King is the world leader in transport refrigeration. They make equipment that keeps food cold, so Jay is proposing the TK Chiller Bowl. Don't forget, films tomorrow at 3:30. We are going to keep our normal routine until we fly out on December 6th. I want to get a couple of practices on that artificial turf. Any questions?"

We leave the Student Union sky-high and immediately go to work on the fundraising party.

To encourage as much participation as possible we come up with the idea to throw parties in both fraternities, ATO and Lambda Chi. A ten-dollar door charge will get you in both houses and all the beer you can drink. While the ten dollar cover is pricey for college students, they enthusiastically support the event to enable the Mules to go bowling.

When Saturday night comes around Tank, Fire Hose and I man the door. We attract a nice crowd. All week we flooded the campuses of both Muhlenberg and Cedar Crest College with flyers. Cedar Crest is an all- women's college that is only a couple miles from Muhlenberg. We also drew interest from a lot of locals with connections to our area undergraduates.

As Robbie Boll and Jon Light walk into our frat the DJ is playing **Love Train** by the O'Jays.

> "People all over the world (everybody)
> Join hands (join)
> Start a love train, love train
> People all over the world (all the world, now)

Join hands (love ride)
Start a love train (love ride), love train"

Robbie inserts his own words as he sings along.

"The next stop that we make will be soon
Tell all the folks in **Minny, and St. Paul**, too
Don't you know that it's time to get on board
And let *the **Mules*** keep on riding, riding on
through
Well, well"

"Nice lyrics Boll-man," I add.

"Yeah, we gonna take the Mule train to Minnesota and run all over the Tommies!" Boll roars.

"Bro, talk up our fundraising activities. We have a kissing booth with our ATO little sisters for dollar kisses in the atrium and a 50/50 raffle floating around," I explain.

"We saw your Tricky Dick dunking booth in the parking lot. I can't believe you recruited guys to sit up there when its 40 degrees out," Jon Light replies with a smirk.

"Well we borrowed a couple of wet suits to make it bearable for the pledges," Tank clarifies.

Our dunk tank event is the brainchild of Scott Cressman. Inspired by President Nixon last Saturday as he gave his "I am not a crook" speech, when he vigorously defended his record in the Watergate case. Most of us booed the TV set as he spoke except for when he discussed energy conservation and made a joke about his efforts to save energy when he refused to allow a back-up aircraft to follow his Air Force Plane. "If this one goes down they don't have to impeach."

Scott bought a Nixon Halloween mask and an Impeach Nixon T-shirt that the pledges wore while Wolfman rented the dunk tank. The entire evening is an awesome experience and a financial success. Nearly eight hundred people partied at the frats and together with the special events we raised over $9,000 after paying for the beer and DJs. We raised almost everything we needed to. Our portion was now down to $30 each. We are on our way.

We arrive in Minnesota on Thursday, December 6th, to three inches of snow on the ground, 19-degree temperatures and a strong north wind. As we deplane we couldn't help but comment on our new environment.

"It is colder than a penguin's pecker," jokes Tank as he descends the mobile stairs onto the tarmac. I can't help but join in as I reply, "Yeah it's so cold I keyed the side of the plane with my nipples." I figured it was best to make a self-imposed, pre-emptive strike and bust my own chops before my teammates do. The guys were always kidding me about my pronounced nipples. They named them diamond-cutters and were unmerciful when I wore tee-shirts.

"It's pretty bad Cobber when we can see your nips through two shirts and an overcoat," Arnie jokes.

After we check into our hotel, we bus over to the University of Minnesota and have a late afternoon practice. Memorial Stadium is totally bitchin'. Especially when compared to our 3,000-seat field. As you approach the front gate you feel like you are going to battle in a

Roman Coliseum. Known as the "Brickhouse", Memorial Stadium is a large brick structure that possess large arched doorways and windows along with a tower anchoring one side.

The locker room is very spacious. Back home we are used to dressing on top of each other but here we each have our own private bench. Plastered all over the stadium is the Thermo King logo with the letters T and K embedded in a crown. The TK Chiller Bowl is an appropriate name for the game given how cold it is in Minnesota in December.

On Friday night, Thermo King Corporation is hosting both teams for a pre-bowl celebration dinner. It's being held at the celebrated Minneapolis Club that was established in 1883. This is one classy joint. The building housing the Club is a huge brick and stone mansion covered in ivy. As we walk through the wood-paneled lobby you sense the historic significance of this stately structure. Presidents and heads of state have dined here and now a bunch of Mules from Allentown, Pennsylvania will break bread in this memorable residence as well.

Dressed in coats and ties, we are on our best behavior. We very much want to make a solid impression on Coach Marino's buddy, Mr. Lamb. Besides the two teams there must have been two hundred guests of Thermo King at the dinner. Mr. Lamb opened the festivities.

"My name is Jay Lamb and I am the Vice President of Sales and Marketing for Thermo King Corporation. I want to extend my sincere welcome to the coaches, players and support staffs of both Muhlenberg College and St. Thomas University. I also want to recognize those

Thermo King Dealers and their family members that have traveled from all over the United States to support this wonderful event. And lastly, but most importantly, I want to acknowledge those guests that are customers of Thermo King Corporation in attendance here tonight. We thank you for making TK the world leader in transport refrigeration since we began in 1938.

Thermo King is a corporation that has built its reputation on quality and excellence. The two teams we have playing in the first ever TK Chiller Bowl embody those qualities as well. Between them they have a combined record of sixteen wins, two defeats and one tie. But beyond success on the playing field these two teams excel in the classroom. Both schools are recognized as two of the finest private academic institutions of higher learning in the country. The men seated before you balance achievement on the gridiron with scholastic success.

We at Thermo King are proud to sponsor the Chiller Bowl and anticipate an exciting game tomorrow. Please enjoy the rest of the evening and take the opportunity to meet these fine young men."

The dinner is enjoyable and I learn more about transport refrigeration than I will ever need to know, but I'm anxious to return to the hotel. My parents and sister flew in today from Jersey and I want to see them tonight, because tomorrow there would be little time before the game for social pleasantries.

We finally finish the evening's celebration and take the team bus back to the hotel. To my surprise my family is sitting in the lobby. My sister greets me with a big hug and kiss. Mom and Dad jump in and we embrace for what seemed to be five minutes.

"It's great to see you son," Mom says.

"I'm glad to see you guys too," I reply. "How was the flight in?"

"Uneventful like it should be," Dad answered.

"Hey Jack, we went over to an indoor shopping center called Southdale. It was far out. There had to be over fifty stores. Do you like this sweatshirt I got?" My sister asks.

"Yeah, it looks way cool on you Judy," I reply.

Dad offers his encouragement, "Jack, make sure you get your rest tonight. I know you are excited about the game but you have to save your energy. Also, win or lose take in the moment. Enjoy every minute of this experience. Few get to do what you are going to do tomorrow. Savor the memories with your teammates. Now get some sleep, we can talk more after the game."

"Good luck tomorrow son. We will be cheering you on. We love you," Mom says supportively.

"Yea brother, don't embarrass our family out there with your "look-out blocks". Hit somebody for a change," My sister wisecracks with comic relief.

"Thanks for the confidence Jude. I'll picture your face on my opponent and that should motivate me," I joked back.

As we warm up on the field the next day the crowd is pouring into Memorial Stadium. I can't help but notice that a sea of purple and white dominates the stands. Those are the Tommie colors. We are situated in St. Thomas's backyard so the crowd is overwhelmingly in their favor among the twelve thousand in attendance. The crowd for the most part was *Minnesota Nice* but a few of the Tommie students carry signs with pictures of donkey rear ends that read, "Kick the Mules Butts" and refer to us as jackasses. Our contingent of Muhlenberg fans numbers about six hundred that journeyed the 1100-mile trip to the Land of Ten Thousand Lakes. They are a small but vocal contingent.

On the sideline, Coach Marino gathers us around the bench and echoes what he emphasized in the pre-game talk. "We need to establish the running game because both teams will be challenged to throw the ball in this cold weather. Again, the team that controls the line of scrimmage and makes the least mistakes will walk away the victor."

Our running game is hitting on all cylinders in the first quarter. We take our second possession and march down the field for a touchdown. Wood scores on a 15-yard drive through the Tommie defense.

The second quarter is a reversal of fortunes as St. Thomas dominates scoring 14 points on a 45-yard punt return and a 21-yard pass interception. Big plays are killing us. In the third quarter, we tie it up at 14-14 when Paul Palmisano catches a 20-yard pass in the corner of the end zone from Fire Hose. On the next series we get two more points when Frankie sacks the Tommie quarterback in the end-zone for a safety. Our 16-14 lead holds up until the St. Thomas kicker converts a 43-yard field goal at the end of the third quarter that makes the score 17-16 in favor of the Tommies.

Most of the fourth quarter is a fierce defensive struggle between both teams. But late in the game, the Tommies go on a sustained drive and move the ball down to our 10-yard line with only a minute and fifteen seconds showing on the clock. Coach Marino calls a timeout and motions the defense to the sideline.

"Listen to me carefully. I want you to let St. Thomas score on the next play. If we don't they can run out the clock on us. Offense, after they score be ready to execute our hurry-up offense," Coach explains.

We couldn't believe what we were hearing, "Let the other team score. What the hell?" It went against all our natural instincts of competition. But the coach knew what he was doing. It was a long-shot, but it was realistically our only chance. St. Thomas has the opportunity to sit on the ball and run out the clock.

On the next play the Tommie halfback sprints around the left end. Our guys make half-hearted attempts to tackle him but he darts unscathed for a touchdown making the score 24-16 after the extra point. The runner didn't realize that it would have been better if he had just fallen to the ground a few yards short of the end zone. With little more than a minute, St. Thomas could have run out the clock by the quarterback taking a knee a few times. But the Tommie halfback's natural instincts took over and he blitzed into the end zone before his intellect could override his desire to score. His intensity didn't allow him to hear his coaches yelling, "Drop down!" The touchdown celebration was cut short as St. Thomas coaches express their concern that the game is not over. The Tommie coaches realize that they had been suckered into this position.

St. Thomas kicks-off and The Jet runs the ball back to our 35-yard line before getting out of bounds. With two timeouts and 65 yards to go for a touchdown we start the drive.

The first play called is a Hook and Ladder trick play. Robbie Boll runs out ten yards along the sideline and hooks in towards the center of the field. Rick Mason hits him with the pass perfectly. As the Tommie tacklers converge on him, Robbie laterals the ball to Jordan Mills who is trailing him. Mills takes the pitch in full stride and ambles another 25 yards before the opposing safety runs him out of bounds. The ball is now situated on the Tommies's 30-yard line. With just under a minute to play and two timeouts, the Coach calls a draw play. Fire Hose drops back to pass and then hands off to our fullback, Woods, who charges through Tommie defenders for ten yards. The ball now rests on the 20-yard line with 50 seconds remaining. After a timeout to stop the clock, a St. Thomas outside linebacker sacks Rick for a five-yard loss. We have to take our last timeout to stop the clock. Coach Marino calls for a jump pass to our tight end. Fire Hose executes the play to perfection. Martinez hikes the ball to Rick from shotgun formation and Fire Hose lofts a beautiful pass to our tight end, Paul Palmisano, in the corner of the left end zone just above the outstretched hands of two St. Thomas defenders. Paul jumps over both d-backs and wrestles the ball away for a touchdown making the score 24-22 in favor of St. Thomas.

We line up for the two-point conversation attempt. Out of shotgun formation Fire Hose rolls to his right executing an option play. With his ends covered he quickly darts to the corner pylon for the tying points. It is the end of regulation time and the score is tied 24-24.

The 600 Muhlenberg fans go wild as the team jumps all over Fire Hose in the end zone as Coach Marino barks out orders to get to the sideline. He is thinking ahead about the overtime session and wants to prepare. Coach knows it's premature to celebrate since we haven't won anything yet.

St. Thomas wins the coin flip and elects to receive the ball in overtime. After a downed kick in the end zone, the Tommies start on their own 20-yard line. They attempt two straight runs that our defense stuffed, only allowing two yards total. With it being third down and eight yards to go for a first down, the Tommie quarterback drops back and attempts a short out pass to his split end. The Jet reads the quarterback's eyes and jumps the pass. He cuts in front of the split end and intercepts the ball. He blazes into the end zone with the winning touchdown. Our entire team mobs him in the end zone. What a complete reversal of fortunes in just over five minutes. St. Thomas must feel like lightning has hit them and in truth it had. It was an abrupt, cruel ending for a team that thought they had salted the bowl game away. However as Yogi Berra, coach of the amazing New York Mets said this past year, "It ain't over til it's over."

As we returned to the sideline Chet, Jon, Chuck and I walk over to Sam Johnson. None of us could hold back the tears as we approach our friend who had taught us to overcome whatever life confronts you with.

"We promised you the game ball when we won the MAC championship. That didn't happen but this is the next best thing. Thanks for showing us what real courage and perseverance look like," Chet said.

"Thanks guys...love y'all," Sam said. Our heads fused together as the five of us celebrated in a tight circle, kissing the ball and each other. It was pure exhilaration and joy. A statement of love for each other, for our college and for the game of football.

After a long and deserving team celebration we walk slowly off the field towards the locker rooms. Debbie broke from the sidelines where she had been performing with the Mule cheerleaders.

"Great game, Jack!" Debbie yells as she jumps up in my arms.

"It was your cheers that made the difference," I reply.

"I love you, Jack Cobb, even though you are a sarcastic twit," Debbie answers back.

"I love you too, Debbie D'Angelo." Just then, my family joined in the hug.

My Dad who is a man that does not dole out compliments easily said, "That was a great game, Jack. I thought all was lost when St. Thomas scored that last touchdown but everything went our way in the last minute. Geeez...that was the most exciting football game I ever saw."

"You played a great game, son. We are so proud of you. Did you hurt anything?" Mom asks in her usual loving manner.

"No Mom, in fact I have never felt better in my life," I respond as I squeeze her in a bear hug.

"How about that winning interception from the Jet? That was a fantastic play. He read the QB's eyes perfectly!" Judy exclaims.

"You got that right. Jet is the man!"

"Does he have a girlfriend?" Judy asks.

"Stop right there, Sis. We're not taking this any further," I state emphatically.

At that moment Coach Marino comes over to greet my family. "Thanks for coming all this way Cobb family," Coach says shaking my Dad's hand and hugging my Mom.

"Great game, Coach," Dad says.

"It's all the boys. They are a great group of young men. They did whatever the coaching staff asked of them all year. Their sacrifices paid off and that's a tribute to the families that raised them," Coach replies.

As thrilled as I was at that moment I couldn't help but see the agony in the eyes of the other team and I couldn't help but think...

There by the grace of God go us.

They had played their hearts out and because of a few critical plays they are feeling total despair. I look over at the St. Thomas bench and notice the linebacker, number fifty-two I had been battling with all afternoon was in tears with his head in his hands. Close to him was a young boy dressed in purple about nine years old in a wheelchair crying his eyes out.

> *It's a damn shame that anyone has to walk off this field today feeling like a loser. Both teams represented themselves admirably and both deserve to celebrate.*

I temporarily broke away from my family and head over to my St. Thomas opponent with my jersey in my hand.

"You guys played a great game today. If not for a few plays we're switching places. And I want you to know that I'll be black and blue for a month from your forearms," I said.

"You guys deserved to win. You never stopped coming at us," replied #52 as he shook my hand.

"If you're cool with it I'd like to trade jerseys with you," I said offering my shirt to him.

"Do it, Tom," said the young boy in the wheelchair.

"It appears my younger brother wants us to exchange. I'd be happy to swap jerseys," explained #52 as he slowly pulled his jersey over his head and handed it to me.

"Thanks...you hang in there," I said as I dropped my jersey in the hands of his younger brother who broke into a smile.

That kid's facial expression meant more to me than anything I saw on the scoreboard today. When you scrape away everything, it's only our interactions with people that really matter. That's what create special moments worthy of lifetime memories.

The next day the Minneapolis Star Newspaper dubbed the game "The Thriller at the Chiller". It was a fantasy finish to an incredible season of ups and downs, but in the end it was a season of redemption. Not lost on me was the fact that the teambuilding and conditioning we did in the summer at the Jersey shore formed the foundation for our turn-around. The crowd cheers evaporated quickly but the relationships and memories were etched in our minds for an eternity.

This was one kick-ass season to remember. Go Mules!

Aftermath:

"What happened to the gang?"

It took five years for **Jack Cobb** to get up the courage to ask **Debbie D'Angelo** to marry him. For a few years Debbie was a professional cheerleader but retired to have four beautiful children with Jack. Jack went on to work for Thermo King Corporation as a teambuilding expert using the lessons he learned at the Jersey Shore.

Wolfman married **Gigi** and had three lovely children in northern New Jersey. He would become partial owner of the New York Giants after making millions in real estate.

The **Palmisano Twins, Chet Stringer and Jack** made it a tradition to meet once a year in Las Vegas to remember the bowl victory and celebrate future triumphs. The Jersey Boys have only been arrested once during their reunion streak.

Arnie Palmisano is a hunting guide and outfitter, spending most of his years in the remote regions of Sweetwater, Wyoming. He lives with his two pet bloodhounds and his significant other, a Native American woman who taught Arnie how to track coyotes.

Chet the Jet Stringer became a professional dancer on Broadway and married the love of his life, Sherry James. They had two beautiful boys who followed their father to the theater.

Jim Shapiro (Tas) finished what he started in Russia and married Chris Ford after graduation. He went on to become an accomplished motivational speaker and exceptional high school wrestling coach. Ten of his student athletes went on to become Pennsylvania state champions.

Paul Palmisano got into hotel management and manages the Barton Creek Resort and Spa in Austin, Texas. He married his masseuse and they had two beautiful kids who look exactly like the mother.

Scott Cressman, Prize Hog became a political columnist for The Philadelphia Inquirer and became the first professional journalist to bench press 500-lbs.

Burt Massa is still living at the ATO fraternity and serves as the permanent chaperone for the house. His time is consumed with lifting weights, ingesting protein supplements and monitoring his vast investment holdings via computer.

Ron Wood went on to medical school and became one of the foremost plastic surgeons in NYC. He married one of his patients and they have six perfect children.

Chuck Biers and **Frankie Johnson** became partners in a construction company that performed most of the fix-up work on the Jersey Parkway. It is rumored that they know where Jimmy Hoffa's body is buried...supposedly near exit 16W off the Jersey Turnpike.

Terry Tank DeStefano went into coaching football. He is now just three victories short of being the all-time leading coach in New Jersey. He was also an early pioneer in full body hair depilation experiments for men.

Robbie Boll lives with his Uncle on LBI and together they own a surf shop. He married Miss Jersey Shore 1982.

Steve "The Preacher" Holland is a missionary in Bulgaria. He puts on wrestling exhibitions and ministers the Word of God afterwards. He married his high school sweetheart and they had three beautiful boys that went on to become accomplished international wrestlers.

Reflections

I would meet up with Billy White Shoes Johnson years later at the Minneapolis Marriot in 2002. At this point, Billy had completed a 15-year career in the NFL and was part of the Atlanta Falcons administrative staff. He had been elected to the College Football Hall of Fame and was also chosen for the NFL's 75th Anniversary All-Time Team. He is considered by many the best punt returner in the history of the game.

The catalyst for our meeting was my youngest child, Hunter. For his seventh birthday I got the family tickets to the Vikings game against the Atlanta Falcons and also made arrangements to stay over at the Downtown Marriot the night before. This game was particularly special because Hunter's favorite team was and still is the Atlanta Falcons.

Little did I know when I made the reservation that the Atlanta Falcons team was scheduled to stay at the Marriot as well. Throughout the evening and the next morning, we encountered several Falcon players in the hotel elevators, the restaurant and common areas including QB Michael Vick, WR Brian Finneran, LB Keith Brooking, CB Ashley Ambrose and CB Ray Buchanan. As you can imagine, Hunter was extremely excited to be that close to his heroes. In fact Ashley and Ray invited him over to their table with their families while they were having breakfast because of his Falcons gear.

To make it even more special for Hunter, Michael Vick set the single game rushing record with 173 yards on 10 carries including the winning 46-yard touchdown run in overtime to lead the Atlanta Falcons to a 30-24 victory over the Vikes...much to my unhappiness.

My surprise thrill took place at the Marriot Gym that Sunday morning before the game. As I ran on the treadmill, Billy Johnson came into the exercise room to workout. I finished my run and went over to the universal equipment. I introduced myself and the fact that we played against each other. We talked for several minutes and a very gracious White Shoes gave me his autograph on Marriot stationery. I was very pleased that one of the greatest NFL players to ever compete on the gridiron considered me a colleague from the old MAC days. Billy is truly a class individual and is one Hot Dog that "can take it as well as he can give it".

The Way We Were

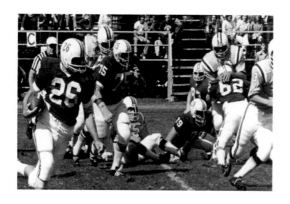

193

GREGORY W. SIDDLER   JEFFREY S. NEIMAN   JAMES A. MURRAY   WILLIAM V. BUTLER JR.   WILLIAM E. WYATT   JAY B. MURRAY

RICHARD R. NIEMIEC   VITALY SAWYNA   DOUGLAS E. CORNWELL   ROBERT W. BUCK   JOHN V. REITZ   JOHN R. GINN

Made in the USA
Monee, IL
15 June 2021